**"Derrick."** The whispered voice over the phone line hit him like a Mack truck.

*Gina.*

"A man is going to kill me unless you help me," she whispered.

"What man?" He came to his feet to pace the deck.

"My brother was murdered. The killer just shot my friend Lilly right in front of me. I grabbed Sophia and ran. Derrick, she's only seven months old. He'll hurt her, too."

The Gina he'd known was calm, levelheaded and not prone to exaggeration. She also didn't panic. Unless the situation called for it. The threat must be real. Unease curdled his stomach. "Where are you?"

"Jantzen Beach."

"I'm on my way."

"Thank you," he heard her say as he disconnected.

Dropping his phone into his pocket, he charged inside and headed straight to his bedroom. He grabbed his gun from the drawer and filled his pocket with ammo.

*Child. Gina has a child.*

A vise gripped his heart. She had a baby. Should've been his child. His daughter.

**Books by Susan Sleeman**

Love Inspired Suspense

  *High-Stakes Inheritance*
  *Behind the Badge*
  *The Christmas Witness*
*Double Exposure*
*Dead Wrong*
*No Way Out*
*Thread of Suspicion*
*Dark Tide*

*The Justice Agency

## SUSAN SLEEMAN

grew up in a small Wisconsin town where she spent her summers reading Nancy Drew and developing a love of mystery and suspense books. Today she channels this enthusiasm into hosting the popular internet website www.thesuspensezone.com and writing romantic-suspense and mystery novels.

Much to her husband's chagrin, Susan loves to look at everyday situations and turn them into murder-and-mayhem scenarios for future novels. If you've met Susan, she has probably figured out a plausible way to kill you and get away with it.

Susan currently lives in Oregon, but has had the pleasure of living in nine states. Her husband is a church music director and they have two beautiful daughters, a very special son-in-law and an adorable grandson. To learn more about Susan, please visit www.SusanSleeman.com.

# ONE

He'd come for her again. Here in the dark—fog oozing over the edge of the floating home's deck and clouding the Columbia River. He'd followed her from San Diego to Portland and burst through the door to her friend Lilly's house. Splintered and hanging by a hinge, it served as a warning of his deadly determination. Gina had stepped out for only a moment, leaving her precious baby niece in her friend's care, and now Sophia and Lilly were helpless inside.

Gina had to rescue them, but how?

She searched the deck, looking for something—anything—she could use to save them. Found only worn patio furniture. No weapons. Nothing to help. Nothing to do.

How could she have been foolish enough not to realize he'd track her down? She should have known that she'd put Lilly at risk by coming to stay with her. And as for Sophia... She'd had custody of her niece for only four months. Not nearly enough time to recover from her brother's death and barely enough time to think of Sophia as her daughter. And now, Gina had put the precious baby in danger.

What if he'd already harmed them? Panic stole her breath.

*Calm down. They're alive and they need you.*

Gina sensed movement on the far end of the deck before rapid footsteps cut through the quiet. She spun and searched the area. The vague outline of a burly man carrying something as he rushed toward the water emerged through the shifting fog.

If Gina could see him, could he see her, too? She flattened her back against the houseboat bobbing in shifting waters.

*Is he carrying a body? Lilly? Oh, God! Please, no!* Despite Gina's prayer, terror crept up her throat and threatened to strangle her.

*Breathe. In. Out. In. Out. That's it. Get it together.*

Now that he was on the deck, it was safe to check inside.

She slipped into the hazy mist rolling over the large deck. One foot in front of the other—feeling her way through murky shadows clinging to the home.

Squinting in the bright light of the family room, she scanned the area. The coffee table and a chair lay discarded on the floor like Sophia's toys, lamp shards scattered nearby. There'd been a struggle.

"Lilly!" Gina called out.

No reply. Fear gaining a stronger hold, Gina hurried toward the bedrooms. She scanned the master. Empty. She charged down the hallway to the room she and Sophia were sharing tonight. A Winnie the Pooh nightlight burned on the far side of the room, not providing enough light for a clear look at her niece.

Holding her breath, Gina rushed to the portable crib.

Sophia slept in her teddy bear pajamas, her tiny bottom up in the air, a Pooh blanket discarded by her feet. Gina pressed her hand on the seven-month-old's back. At the even rise and fall, Gina sagged against the crib.

*Thank You, God.*

She hadn't failed her brother. Sophia was safe.

*Lilly. Where is Lilly?* The thought barreled into Gina's brain.

Lilly would never leave Sophia alone. Never.

Had her attacker taken Lilly, hoping Gina would swap places to save Lilly's life?

Gina bolted through the house and back outside. A scraping noise ground against the end of the deck, followed by a loud thump.

Holding her breath, she crept over the slippery planks to the back of the house and listened. The river lapped against floating homes, but another noise broke the gentle rhythm—the dunk then pull of oars whispering through the night.

To gain a clearer view, she took a few more steps toward the water and saw the stern of a small boat rowed by a large man moving away. He wasn't masked as he'd been last night, but he was the right size and build for the man who'd attacked her.

The boat stopped, and he stood then heaved an anchor into the water. He braced his feet wide then bent low and dragged a body from the boat.

*Lilly. Oh, no.*

He lifted her like a rag doll and pinned her against his wide chest. He drew a gun from his belt and pressed the barrel against her temple.

*No!*

Was he going to kill her? Or did he know Gina was watching and he hoped she'd show herself? She had to risk it. She ran to the edge of the deck to order him to stop and take her instead.

The gun flashed and a pop split the silence.

Lilly's body sagged. The man released her, and she dropped like an anchor into the water. He stood looking down at the spot where Lilly had fallen.

He'd shot Lilly. Killed her.

A strangled cry came from Gina's mouth, and she took a step back. Her heel connected with a table, knocking a container to the deck. The metallic *clang, clang, clang* as it rolled over the wood cut through the night, and the man's head popped up.

She scrambled back into the shadows. He'd killed Lilly. Right in front of her. Shot her.

Gina dropped her head low and breathed deep to stem a wave of nausea. Still gagging, she watched the man.

He holstered his gun and started drawing up his

anchor. Hand over hand, he moved at a fast clip. He'd seen her and was coming for her next. For Sophia.

*No!*

Gina charged inside the home. She grabbed her overnight bag and slung the strap across her chest. She scooped up Sophia, Pooh blanket and all. The baby startled for a moment, and Gina hugged her close, laying her cheek against soft curls for the briefest of moments. Her sweet baby sighed then drifted back to sleep.

Back on the deck, Gina heard the man's oars hitting the water. *Plop, swish. Plop, swish,* he moved steadily closer. She had to hurry.

She raced toward the dock, clutching Sophia in one arm and digging out her phone to call 9-1-1 with her free hand.

"Help," she whispered so the man couldn't hear her. "I need help." She blurted out her story as she heard his boat thump against the end of the deck.

"Hurry. Send someone fast. He's right behind me. Closing in on me faster than I'd thought." She huffed out Lilly's address, but she could no longer carry on a conversation and pull in enough air to run. She shoved the phone in her pocket and charged toward the gangplank that connected this small floating village with the shore.

In the parking lot, she wished for her car, but she'd flown to Portland and arrived at Lilly's house by taxi. She ran as hard as she could, her feet pounding toward the nearby mall.

Heavy footfalls soon slapped on the asphalt in the distance behind her. She had to hide and hope the police arrived on time. At the nearest store, she sank into the shadows of a large Dumpster.

A foghorn sounded from the river.

Fog. What about the fog? Wouldn't it slow down the police response? She couldn't risk them not arriving in time. She had to summon more help. Preferably someone nearby.

*Derrick.*

Thankful a mutual friend had shared his cell number just after she'd arrived in town, she dialed the phone.

*Please answer, Derrick. Please. I need you.*

The thought took the last shred of her calm. She didn't want to need him or anyone else. Didn't deserve his help with the way she'd walked out on him. But she trusted him to come through for her, whether she deserved it or not. Life-and-death matters trumped pride. He'd balk at helping, but he was a man of honor. Of integrity. One who worked hard to find justice for the underdog. He'd never let her down. No matter what she'd done to him in the past.

As reality settled in, her stomach cramped hard. Sophia's and her own life now depended on the very man who never wanted to see her again.

From the upper deck of Derrick Justice's houseboat, he stared over the Columbia River, letting the rhythmic flow of the river melt away his terrible day.

Okay, so maybe it hadn't been terrible. Just stressful. Something he never thought he'd say about an early dinner with his siblings, but since they'd all married, he felt out of place at family gatherings.

"Get used to it," he mumbled to himself. *You're not marriage material. This is your life now.* A life that would be filled with watching all of them making doe eyes at each other and playing touchy-feely. It was enough to gag him.

The hardest to take was his twin, Dani. He'd always been able to count on her to stand in solidarity with him. But now, she'd gone to the other side, too. In the two months since she'd married Luke Baldwin, Derrick had hardly seen her outside of work at the family's private investigation agency.

He drew in a deep breath, let it out and watched the vapor swirl up then disappear into the haze. He propped his arms behind his head and noticed long fingers of the fog creep over the edge of his second-story deck. Soon it would surround him and he wouldn't be able to see a thing. Perfect. Just the way he wanted it tonight.

His phone chimed. He glanced at the screen. Not someone he knew, but the call could be related to a case so he answered. "Derrick Justice."

"Derrick." The whispered voice hit him like a Mack truck, and air whooshed out of his lungs. He shook his head in disbelief.

Was it really her, or had all these thoughts of marriage parading through his head tonight unearthed a memory he'd rather avoid? Holding his breath, he waited for her to speak again.

"Derrick, are you there?" Her voice was stronger this time.

*Gina.*

A chill settled over him, and he thought about hanging up. He didn't need to talk to the woman who'd walked out on him. Especially not today when he was already crabby about family members leaving him behind.

"A man is going to kill me unless you help me," she whispered.

"What man?" He came to his feet to pace the deck.

"My brother was murdered. The killer just shot my friend Lilly right in front of me. I grabbed Sophia and ran. Derrick, she's only seven months old. He'll hurt her, too. I can't fail her. But he's…" Her voice fell off in a strangled sob.

The Gina he'd known was calm, levelheaded and not prone to exaggeration. Self-reliant, asking for help only as a last resort. She also didn't panic. Unless the situation called for it. The threat must be real.

Unease curdled his dinner. "Where are you?"

"Jantzen Beach. I'm hiding behind Coffee to Go's Dumpster."

"Did you call the police?"

"Yes, but I'm afraid the fog will slow them down and they won't get here in time."

"I'm on my way. Make sure your phone is set to vibrate so it won't be heard if I need to call you."

"Thank you," he heard her say as he disconnected.

Dropping his phone in his pocket, he charged inside and headed straight to his bedroom. He grabbed his gun from the drawer and filled his pocket with ammo. No telling how much he might need.

On the way to the main door, he snatched his car keys from a hook. Running cross-country would be faster than getting his car out of the garage and driving, but he'd need his car to pull off the safe rescue of a woman with a child.

*Child. Gina has a child.*

A vice gripped his heart. She had a baby. Should've been his child. His daughter.

"Too bad," he mumbled as he climbed into his SUV. *She didn't want you, now, did she?*

Once on the road to the mall, doing fifty in a thirty-five zone, he speed-dialed Dani. It was foolhardy enough to go into a dangerous situation without backup, but the situation was too dangerous for him to wait. Still, he needed to let one of his siblings know where he was going.

"Derrick," she answered on the third ring.

He quickly explained the situation. "Gina called the police, but this is a potential homicide, so call Mitch, too." Their sister, Kat's, husband was a Portland homicide detective. "I'll call you as soon as I have anything else to report."

"Be careful."

"Always."

He turned into the strip mall's lot, his focus going

straight to the coffee shop at the far end of the mall. Hazy mist clung to the concrete, inching up the siding as if planning to devour it, while windows on the darkened stores stared blankly back at him. He crawled through the lot, not spotting any movement.

Had Gina fabricated this incident? Played him? If so, what did she want with him? Only one way to find out.

He parked at the end of the building and got out. He drew his weapon, and after a careful sweep of the area, rounded the corner. Sliding along the building to protect his back, he glanced into the service alley. Light filtered through the moisture-laden air from a streetlight in the distance, but nothing moved. He chanced a longer look, and once he was confident he wouldn't be ambushed, he flattened his back against the wall again and eased toward the Dumpster.

Toward Gina.

A few more steps took him to the back side of the metal container angled against the building. In the corner, large, terrified eyes peered up at him. Eyes he'd stared into for two years in college and once figured he spend his life looking into.

*Gina.*

She cowered in the corner, a sleeping baby clutched to her chest.

"Derrick," she whispered, her voice trembling.

She wasn't faking her terror. Someone *was* after her, and she needed him.

*Correction. She needs your help, not you.*

The thought helped him steel himself for her touch, and he offered his hand. As he'd expected, when she slipped soft fingers into his, it burned all the way to his heart. Their eyes met and held. He suddenly wanted to let go of common sense, of their past, the pain and heartache, and draw her into a comforting hug to erase the misery from her eyes.

She shivered violently, pulling her gaze free, breaking the intensity of the moment and bringing him back to his senses. She wore only a heavy sweater and jeans. Shrugging out of his jacket, he settled it over her shoulders. She burrowed into the fleece lining without a word.

"Are you okay?" he asked.

"It's a long story. Can we get out of here before I explain?"

He opened his mouth to agree, but something rustled behind him and he spun to search the area. Darkness met his gaze—he saw no one. But then heavy footsteps pulled his focus to the distance. They pounded nearer, their cadence laden with caution.

*The killer? Of course. Who else would it be on a night like this and after the mall has closed?*

"He's coming. We have to move." Derrick scanned the alley for an escape route. Nothing presented itself without leaving them exposed. If the footsteps belonged to the man trailing Gina, they were trapped.

Derrick needed a plan and needed one fast. He grabbed Gina's arm and pulled her from behind the Dumpster, a surefire death trap if the killer caught them back here. He looked around, his mind waffling as he decided what to do.

The footfalls neared, echoing into the night before disappearing.

Derrick had to act. Now! Even if he failed.

He drew Gina down the alley then moved her into an alcove and settled her back against the wall. He stepped in front of her, hiding her from the attacker's view, his back to the killer. He didn't like exposing his back, but what else could he do? He had to protect her and the baby from the killer. At any cost. Even his life.

"Lower the baby and put her between us," he whispered, wondering how Gina was going to take the next part of his makeshift plan.

Her eyes wide and darkening with fear, she complied, hugging her child to her chest without taking her focus from him.

He was tempted to lift his hand and cup her face—to comfort her—but that would lead his emotions in a direction he couldn't go. Wouldn't go, especially when he needed to stay focused. He had to keep his mind on the man pursuing her. "I'm going to kiss you and hope this guy thinks we're having a little fun back here."

"But—" She tried to ease away.

Footsteps closed in on them, now only a few yards away. Derrick held his gun at the ready while sliding his other hand into the soft silkiness of her hair to stop her from squirming away. Keeping enough distance between them so the baby could breath, he lowered his head. Gina closed her eyes, the long lashes settling on high cheekbones.

At the touch of their lips, years melted away and he was instantly back at Southern Oregon University the night before she'd left in their senior year. Her citrus scent wrapped around him, and it took everything he was made of not to deepen the kiss.

With sheer force of will, he pulled his mind from her and watched out of the corner of his eye. A figure emerged from the fog yet hung back in the building's shadows. Tall and bulky, he stilled his feet at the sight of them, darkness fully cloaking his face.

Derrick felt the man's eyes linger on them. He gripped his gun tighter, his finger on the trigger, ready to use. His muscles tensed as he waited for a bullet to fly through the night. But he stayed his course, even when a crash of adrenaline urged him to flee.

Suddenly the man huffed out of the shadows. Six-two, maybe three, he wore an oversize jacket, his hood up. He focused on his feet as he walked and pulled the hood tighter to his face, preventing Derrick from catching any identifying features. He hurried past them and down the alley.

If Derrick was alone he'd go after the man, but he had Gina and a baby to think of. *Gina.* She was here now. In front of him. Connected to him.

He lifted his head. When her eyes fluttered open, he stared into the warm brown color and wondered what to do next. The danger of a gunshot may have passed, but it had taken only one kiss to expose his heart to a danger he'd barely survived once and wasn't sure he'd survive again.

# TWO

Shaken, Gina let Derrick hurry her through the spitting rain to his SUV.

"Normally I'd wait for the police to arrive," he said as he opened the passenger door. "But your attacker is still in the area, and it's better to move you to a safe location."

She climbed in and settled Sophia on her lap. Her hands trembled as she tightened the Pooh blanket around the sleeping child.

She'd opened her eyes in time to see Lilly's killer in the alley. He'd come close—too close. The sight of him had frightened her enough to close her eyes again and lean farther into the man shielding her. If not for Derrick…

A shudder claimed her body and she forced the thought away. He *had* responded and he was here now. That was all that mattered.

She watched him run around the front of his vehicle, the streetlight highlighting his sandy-blond hair. He carried himself with more confidence than she remembered, and when the creep had closed in on them, she'd seen an internal strength Derrick hadn't possessed in college.

Jaw clamped tight, he slid behind the wheel and jerked his door closed with a resounding thud. He was angry or irritated or both. He didn't say a word but cranked the engine and shifted into gear. Sophia stirred and Gina stroked her back. How close Gina had come to losing her.

She bowed her head. *Thank You for keeping her safe, Father. Please keep watching over her. Over us.*

Derrick clicked on the signal, drawing her attention.

She looked around. "Where are we going?"

"We'll start by driving around to make sure we've lost him. Then head to my place to regroup." He turned onto a major street.

Gina suddenly realized Sophia wasn't in a car seat. "I'm grateful for your help, Derrick, more grateful than you know, but I don't want to take Sophia on a highway without a car seat. Can you please stay on side streets?"

"I won't leave the area," he said, not bothering to look at her.

He clearly wasn't glad to see her, but then she'd expected that reaction. She hadn't expected this terrible remorse for asking for his help when she'd treated him so poorly to well up and bring tears to her eyes. Being a stand-up guy, he had no alternative but to come to her rescue. She knew she'd put him in a difficult position.

Could she let him assist them under those conditions? Could she afford not to, despite the way she felt? Given any other choice, she'd handle this herself as she did everything else in life, but she couldn't risk Sophia's life.

Like it or not, she needed him to protect them. Plus he could help find her brother, Jon's, killer.

She glanced at the set of his jaw, his rigid posture. Still, she wanted him to *choose* to help them and not feel forced into it by his chivalrous nature. Now that the immediate danger had passed, she needed to give him an easy out.

Praying he wouldn't actually take her up on her offer, she faced him. "You could drop us off at the nearest MAX station and I can—"

"You're kidding, right?" He whipped his head around to stare at her. "A man kills your friend then comes after you, and you think I'm going to drop you off at a public train station? Un-be-lievable."

"Once you're sure he hasn't followed us, we should be safe until I can find another investigator." She tried to imbue her voice with her usual confidence, but she couldn't manage it.

"Look." Derrick tightened his fingers around the steering wheel. "I get that you don't want to be around me, but I'm not letting you out of my sight until I know you're okay. So sit back and relax while I keep a watch on the streets." He jerked a hand free and cranked up the heater.

Sit back and relax—right. Like she could unwind when a man had tried to kill her. Twice. Or chill out in any way with Derrick at her side. She'd gotten what she'd wanted, though. He'd willingly agreed to help them, but that meant they'd be thrown together and clearly he still had an effect on her.

Sophia shifted and Gina knew she owed it to the baby to at least try to calm down. If she didn't, she'd burn out, and Sophia needed her. She concentrated on the heat flowing under the dash. The temperature had dipped a good ten degrees below normal February temperatures from what she could remember of her college days in Oregon. She moved her soaked shoes under the flowing air, then settled deeper into Derrick's jacket and inhaled his woodsy scent clinging to it.

She drifted back to their college days. To that last day. Breaking up. Saying goodbye. Her heart a mass of pain.

What would her life have been like if she hadn't broken things off with him? Would Derrick have stood by her when Jon died, leaving Gina to raise Sophia alone, or would he have run like her recent ex-fiancé, Ben?

*Waste of time to think about it.*

Sure, they'd loved each other in college, but she'd soon learned that he couldn't commit to a long-term relationship. Why, she wasn't sure, and it didn't matter. Men who couldn't commit and broken promises were the story of her life. Starting with her minister father, whose church was more important than her. Always more important. Then Derrick and Ben.

Three strikes and she was out. She was over trying to find a man who'd be there for her. So over it.

*It's been nine years. Maybe Derrick changed.*

Didn't matter. Not even if she *was* interested. And after Ben's recent rejection, she wasn't interested in any man.

Besides, Derrick had likely gotten over his commitment issues and was married with kids. She glanced at his hand to see if he wore a wedding ring, but he'd dropped it from the wheel and out of view.

Just as well.

She didn't need to be pondering his marital status anyway. She turned away and watched the lush scenery as they drove around the area. After fifteen minutes, Derrick pulled up to a long row of garages for houseboat owners. He pressed the remote clipped on the visor, sending the end door rumbling up. Once inside, he sat staring ahead, as if unsure how to proceed. The awkward silence grew, and she searched for something to say. But what could she say?

*Sorry I bailed on you, on us, but now that I need you, please be there for me.*

Hardly.

He drew in a long breath and exhaled as if he needed to fortify himself just to look at her before swiveling to face her. "If I'm going to help you, I need to ask a few questions."

"Okay," she said hesitantly. Did he intend to ask about their past?

"Tell me about tonight. About your friend. Give me exact details."

She rubbed hard calluses on her fingers from playing violin, the feeling familiar and comforting as she recounted the terrifying ordeal on Lilly's boat as matter-of-factly as possible. "I can't be positive the woman he shot was Lilly, but she'd never willingly leave Sophia alone."

"Must've been hard to lose her like that." He lifted a hand, reaching for her as if he planned to touch her then dropped it to his knee.

"I keep hoping she survived."

He lifted his hand again, and she was surprised at how much she wanted to feel his comforting touch, but he dug out his phone instead. "Kat's husband, Mitch, is a homicide detective. Dani has already called him about your attack. If you give me Lilly's address, I'll have him head over there instead of to the mall."

"Homicide?" she asked, hating the finality of the word. "But what if I was wrong and Lilly's alive?"

"Even if she survived, which from the scene you described is not very likely, the investigation will be handled as an attempted murder, which means Mitch will work the case."

His brutal honesty when she wanted comfort felt like a slap in the face, and she jerked back.

"Look." His eyes softened. "I'm sorry for being so blunt, but I don't want you to hold on to unrealistic hope."

He was right. She had to face this just like she'd faced Jon's death and the attack in San Diego. Like she'd faced leaving Derrick so long ago. With courage and bravery. Sophia was counting on her. She had to be strong.

She rattled off Lilly's address and Derrick phoned his brother-in-law. She listened to his conversation and heard the professional lingo of a former cop roll off his tongue. She pictured him as an officer who would be compassionate, caring, yet hard-nosed and one who would fight for justice. For the downtrodden, as he'd chosen to do early in life after the drunk driver who killed his birth parents got off with a slap on the wrist. He'd even majored in criminal justice in college.

Though she hadn't been in touch with him since college, she'd kept tabs on him through mutual friends. She knew about the years he'd served as a police officer—and the decision he'd made to leave that career behind after his adoptive parents were killed. Along with his twin and his three adopted siblings, he'd formed a private investigation agency, first to find the people responsible for their parents' deaths, and then to help others in need. And now he was helping her.

"Thanks, Mitch." He disconnected and stowed the phone. "He'll check out Lilly's house. We can wait inside to hear back from him." Derrick paused and seemed to consider his next words carefully. "I don't think we were tailed, but we'll pretend we're on a date again while we walk in. Just in case."

She opened her mouth to protest, and he flipped up his hand. "Don't worry. I won't kiss you again. But I *am* going to put my arm around you, and you'll have to suffer my touch one more time." He jerked open his door and quickly climbed out as if he needed to get away from her.

She shifted Sophia to her shoulder, and as she stepped down from his SUV, she grabbed his jacket. When she joined him at the door, he took the jacket and covered Sophia then slipped his arm around her back. His warmth seeped into her body and, she hated to admit, the attraction she'd felt since the first day she'd seen him in psychology class seeped into her heart.

He didn't seem to notice. His eyes alert and watchful, he hurried them through the lot and across the gangway to a floating home much larger than Lilly's boat. Inside, Gina took a moment to look around. She'd once thought floating homes were cramped like a boat, but in Derrick's home, floor-to-ceiling windows made the room look large and inviting. The spacious kitchen with full-size appliances and connected to a large family room made it feel like a regular house.

He crossed to a gray sectional and shoved a padded ottoman into the corner. "Your daughter should be fine on the sofa as long as one of us is in the room."

"About that," she said, feeling a need to clarify. "Sophia is my niece—Jon's daughter. His wife died in a car crash when she was seven months pregnant, but they were able to save Sophia. I stepped in to help raise her. When Jon also died a few months ago…" Feeling no need to elaborate, she quit speaking.

"I'm sorry for your loss." His words carried an understanding that came from losing his parents when he was not even eleven years old.

"Thank you," she said and quickly moved on before she started getting weepy. "I'm thinking the man who attacked me tonight is the same man who killed Jon. I was hoping you'd help me find him."

Derrick ran a hand over his damp hair that curled at the edges and seemed to mull it over. She caught sight of his bare ring finger and immediately squelched the joy that knowing he was single brought.

"Since this is going to be a long discussion," he finally said, "I'm gonna put on a dry shirt and get one for you before we get started." He didn't wait for agreement before turning away. As he climbed the stairs, he pulled out his phone and called his sister Dani.

True to course, he phoned his twin whenever he had a big decision to make. Apparently he hadn't changed after all. After her unexpected reaction to discovering he was single, she'd best watch herself or she'd find herself falling for him all over again.

And she'd be hurt again. After so much pain in her life already.

She pressed a kiss on Sophia's downy curls. A moment of sadness lingered for all they'd both lost. Her sister-in-law dying, Jon's murder. Now Lilly.

Tears Gina had kept at bay since last night burned at the back of her eyes, and she hugged Sophia tighter. When she heard Derrick pad down the stairs, she forced down her grief.

If she'd learned anything from her father's lack of affection and from men who couldn't put her first in life, it was never to let them see her vulnerability.

After settling Sophia on the sofa, Gina watched as Derrick came into the room wearing a body-hugging T-shirt and a deep scowl. One hand shoved in his pocket, he carried a worn flannel shirt in the other. When he got close enough, he tossed it to her as if he hated to think of touching her again.

"I'll keep an eye on Sophia while you change. There's a bathroom down the hall." He tipped his head at a hallway near the far end of the family room.

She clutched the nubby fabric that smelled just like him and hurried to the bathroom, where she stripped off her shirt. Her eyes drifted to the mirror and fixed on the large purple bruise on her shoulder courtesy of last night's attack. She quickly slipped into Derrick's shirt and hugged the comforting fabric close. She didn't like their past issues adding turmoil to this already difficult situation. Still, she lifted her head and prayed that Derrick would stay close by so the man who'd put this ugly bruise on her shoulder and likely killed Jon and Lilly wouldn't come anywhere near her or her beloved little Sophia again.

"C'mon, Dani," Derrick whispered under his breath as he made a cup of tea for Gina. "Get here already."

Gina's tea was nearly ready, and if he lingered in the kitchen any longer, she'd figure out he was stalling so he could avoid her. It was for her own good. He couldn't look at her and not remember what they'd once had. Something he still wanted in his life but couldn't grab hold of.

After her traumatic day, the last thing she needed was to deal with their past. She deserved to be treated with kid gloves right now. Her situation roused all his protective instincts and he wanted to be there for her, but he didn't know if he could do it.

*What's a guy supposed to do in a situation like this, God? Should I run as fast I can in the other direction? Let her find someone else to help as she offered to do?*

He looked over the large island to the family room, where she changed Sophia's diaper. She wore his shirt buttoned up to the neck, giving a break to her black attire. A music major in college, she'd worn bold colors and bright patterns to complement her artistic flair. Never black. Maybe she'd changed, or maybe she'd dressed this way not to draw attention.

She got up from the couch, Sophia in one arm, and held out the dirty diaper. "Do you have a trash can outside for this?"

He nodded and before he could offer to dispose of it for her, she settled Sophia into his arms. "I'll be right back."

He gaped after her and jiggled the baby. He could count on one hand the number of times he'd held a baby. Wouldn't even take half of his fingers. Maybe he should put her on the sofa. Wouldn't want to break her or anything.

He was moving cautiously toward the family room when the patio door slid open.

Dani stepped inside and her jaw dropped. "You didn't mention a baby."

"I didn't know what to tell you." He quickly off-loaded Sophia onto Dani and sighed out a breath of relief. "She's Gina's niece. Her brother, Jon's, child, but she has custody of her."

Dani arched a brow.

"I'll make sure she explains it when we question her. Just be patient."

"Me, patient?" She laughed and dropped onto the sofa. She put Sophia on her lap and cooed at the child. Eliciting no response, Dani patted her chubby hands together, something Derrick would never think to do.

"What's your name, little one?" Dani asked in a high voice.

"Sophia," Derrick answered.

"Well, hello, Sophia." A goofy smile claimed Dani's face. With looks like that, it wouldn't be long before she had a family of her own.

Sophia grinned, revealing one tooth on the bottom, and despite Derrick's lack of knowledge about babies, he found himself smiling back. Until the door opened. Then he tensed and waited for Gina to join them. He heard water running in the guest bath and knew she'd stopped to wash her hands. When she did enter the room and spotted Dani, a quick flash of unease crowned on her face. She probably thought Dani would let her have it for bailing on him all those years ago.

Maybe she would. Although Dani was his twin and they often thought on the same wavelength, he never knew what was going to come out of her mouth.

"Hello, Dani." Gina marched purposefully across the room. Her strength even in the face of potential adversity didn't surprise him in the least. Her vulnerability in the car, though—that's what got to him.

Dani looked up, and Derrick could feel her demeanor change from across the room.

"Gina." A sharp edge cooled her voice. "Long time no see."

"It has been a while for sure." Gina's tone was far warmer than Dani's, but then she didn't have a twin brother who'd been summarily dumped. "I didn't realize you were coming over."

Dani cast an irritated look at Derrick, who shrugged in reply.

"No biggie," he said. "It just didn't come up."

The teakettle trilled from the kitchen, and he escaped his twin's glare to turn it off. He poured steaming water over a fragrant chamomile tea bag Dani had left in his cupboards. He kept an ear on their conversation—it seemed to be centering on babies and Dani's recent marriage—and carried a mug for Gina and Dani to the family room.

"You mentioned your brother had been murdered," he said, directing them away from the baby talk so they could create a plan to keep Gina safe. When her smile fell, he instantly regretted his blunt choice of words.

As he sat next to Dani, she socked him in the arm. "Tactful, sport. Real tactful."

Normally he'd spar with Dani, but she was right. He was going out of his way to deny the attraction he still felt for Gina to the point of being rude. But what else could he do? He couldn't follow his interest and pretend things would be different this time. She'd hurt him when she'd left, but he'd hurt her first when he hadn't been able to commit long-term. Nothing had changed in his life. He still choked at the thought of a lifetime commitment.

So he had to get a handle on his feelings. How, he didn't know. The only thing he did know for certain right now was if he let this connection that still existed between them continue to get the best of him, he'd hurt her again. And no man worth his salt would intentionally hurt a woman—or stand by and let her get hurt. So if someone really was after her, he'd have to protect her.

No matter how much it would hurt to have her back in his life…and then let her go again.

# THREE

"It's okay, Gina, take your time." Dani's eyes, blue as her designer shirt, never left Gina. "We're here to help when you're ready to talk about it."

Gina tried to let the comfort of Dani's tone take away her tension, but she could feel Derrick watching her from the arm of a leather chair, and his scrutiny made her nervous. She willed herself not to look at him and cleared her throat before beginning. "This all started with my brother, Jon. He was a member of the Coast Guard's Pacific Tactical Law Enforcement Team stationed in San Diego."

"Wow," Derrick interrupted. For the first time his face appeared animated. "That's a pretty exclusive job. Only the best of the best are chosen for those teams."

"I'm surprised you've heard of them," Gina said. "Most people don't know anything about the teams."

"I've read about their successes over the years. I find it fascinating. Traveling the globe. Fighting the war on drugs and smuggling."

Right. A carefree life. No strings, no attachments. A job like that would probably be perfect for Derrick.

"Well, I haven't heard of them," Dani said. "I didn't even know the Coast Guard stationed people outside the country."

Gina nodded. "Oddly enough, they deploy on Navy ships and go wherever needed. They board suspected drug dealers' and smugglers' boats, arrest the criminals then turn them over to the authorities and move on. They can be gone more than two hundred days a year."

"So they're like the cops of the water?" Derrick clarified.

"Yes, except they don't do any of the investigative work on the cases. The Coast Guard team solely handles the arrests."

"Would be hard to be married to a man gone so often." Dani stared into the distance.

Gina was sure Dani was thinking about how hard it would be to leave her new husband, and a flash of jealousy bit into Gina at how deeply dedicated the woman seemed to be to her marriage. If Derrick had shown the willingness to make that kind of pledge to her…but he hadn't. She forced her mind back on her story. "It takes a big commitment and one Jon was looking to move out of after Sophia was born."

Gina's voice faltered as she thought about what came next in her story. "His wife, Becki, was in a terrible car crash last year. She was seven months pregnant at the time. She didn't survive, but fortunately they were able to save Sophia."

Dani slid forward and squeezed Gina's hand. "I'm so sorry. That must've been rough. Especially with your brother's frequent deployments."

"Thankfully he was on leave while Sophia was in the neonatal unit at the hospital. But once she was healthy enough to come home, I moved in to take care of her. Since I was on summer break from teaching, he went back to his team until he could push through the paperwork to officially resign."

"So you're a music teacher like you'd always dreamed?" Derrick asked.

"Yes," she answered, wondering if Derrick ever missed a thing anyone said. "I'm a high school orchestra director. At least, I hope I'm still employed after my hasty departure."

"I'm sure they'll understand." Dani slid back in her seat and draped an arm over the sofa. "So was your brother killed on duty?"

"No. He died in a car crash just a few miles from our apartment."

"Just like his wife," Derrick mumbled to himself.

"No, not like Becki at all," Gina snapped then instantly felt bad about it. "Sorry. I shouldn't have reacted like that, but I'm certain Jon was murdered. Becki was simply late for a doctor's appointment so she was driving recklessly. She lost control and hit a telephone pole. From that day on Jon drove like a little old man. Slow and cautiously. The police say he was speeding and lost control near a cliff. I know better. He would never want to leave Sophia without a father, too. If he lost control of the car, someone must have tampered with it."

"That should be easy to prove," Derrick said. "Didn't the police conduct an investigation?"

Gina faced him, making sure she conveyed the same tenacity she'd once hoped would convince the San Diego detective to keep looking into Jon's case. "They say they did, but if so, how could they reach this conclusion? It just doesn't make any sense. And I told them that. I kept after them until they finished the investigation and handed me his personal possessions." She shook her head. "They were so terse. Like they were glad to be rid of him. Or maybe rid of me. It's almost like they were covering something up and couldn't wait to close the case and move on."

Dani peered at Derrick, and they shared a look that Gina couldn't read.

Were they like the police—doubting her story?

She sat up straighter. "I know you're both thinking I'm a crazed sister who can't accept that her brother is gone. But that's not true. I had to let his loss go. For Sophia. But I can't let go of my belief that the police are wrong and he was murdered."

"Um, actually," Dani said with a smile, "I was thinking you were a conspiracy theory nut."

Despite the tension cutting through the room, Gina laughed. Dani always had a way of lightening things up even in the most difficult of circumstances.

"I haven't gone off the deep end…" Gina offered Dani an exaggerated wink "…yet."

"But you think the police are lying to you." Derrick's humorless tone killed the mood.

Gina shouldn't have expected him to laugh with her, but his continued tight-lipped approach hurt. "Maybe they're not lying to me, but after I was attacked in my apartment last night by a man who was looking for Jon's flash drive, I know I'm not wrong that there's more to his death than meets the eye."

"Back up," Derrick nearly shouted as he came to his feet. "You were attacked last night?"

"Yes. A masked man broke in—I'm almost certain it's the same man who attacked Lilly and tried to chase me down tonight. He wanted a flash drive that was in the box the police had given to me. I was terrified for Sophia, so I gave it to him. I thought he'd take it and run. But he said I could've looked at the files on it, so he had to kill me." Sophia whimpered and Gina leaned over to rub her back.

Derrick's nose flared in anger. "How did you get away?"

"He pulled his trigger. The firing pin jammed. Jon made sure I kept a gun in the nightstand during his deployments, so I ran for it. The man kept coming at me. I fired in his direction, and he took off." Though she was able to keep her emotions in check long enough to tell her story, a long shiver worked over her body, and she wrapped her arms around her stomach for comfort.

"*Did* you look at the files on the flash drive?" Derrick asked.

"Yes, but the only thing other than photos I took of Sophia was a log of some sort. It looked like someone snapped a picture of the document. Only the bottom part of it showed up, so I don't have a clue what it was for."

Derrick perched on the arm again and leaned forward. "I'm assuming you called the police after you were attacked and told them about the flash drive and the log."

She nodded, moving back from his intense stare. "Not that it did me any good. I only glanced at the log, so I wasn't able to tell them much about it."

"If the detectives on Jon's case didn't back you up on the log then that must mean they didn't look at the flash drive when they had it in their possession."

"You know, I never asked," Gina said. "But Jon hid the flash drive in a wooden cross that he wore around his neck. The police may not have even realized the drive was there. I doubt they thought it was more than a religious symbol, and they probably didn't bother to examine it very carefully. Especially when they believed his death was accidental."

Derrick arched his brow. "Why did he feel a need to hide his drive?"

She hated admitting this, but she had to tell the truth. "Rules prohibited him from carrying a flash drive on board. Guess the Navy worried about secrets being stolen or something."

Dani nodded. "It's a problem."

Derrick gave his twin a fond smile. "And as our agency's computer expert, she would know."

"Well, Jon didn't steal anything. He just wanted to have a way to keep current pics of Sophia with him during long deployments. They had computers on the ship for personal use, but they didn't have internet access. So whenever they docked, he downloaded to his drive the pictures that I posted online." She paused. "I know he was violating the rules, but after losing Becki, he needed these pictures to keep going."

"Did you explain this to the police the night of your attack?" Derrick asked.

"Yes, but there weren't any signs of a forced entry or odd fingerprints in my apartment, so they doubted my story. There was a bit of blood on the floor—I think I may have shot him—but they said it wasn't enough blood for a gunshot injury and that maybe Jon had just cut himself weeks before, and I hadn't noticed the blood until now."

"So they stopped investigating?"

"Not until they called the detective working Jon's case, and he told them I was a nutcase. That I'd hounded them all the time when they were already doing their jobs. He suggested I faked the attack to get them to reopen Jon's case." Despite wanting to remain calm and in control, Gina trembled.

"Do you have any idea of your attacker's identity?" Dani asked.

"I don't know," Gina answered hesitantly. She hated to direct suspicion at Jon's best friend.

Derrick eyed her for a moment. "That wasn't very convincing. Is there something you're not telling us?"

"No... I mean..." She shrugged. "I'm not sure about this, and I hate to cast doubt on a family friend."

"I know this is hard, Gina." Dani sat forward again. "But you'll have to bare your soul to us if you don't want your attacker to go unpunished."

Dani was right. Finding Jon's killer plus making sure she and Sophia stayed safe were the most important things. "Jon's friend and teammate Quentin Metzger lives next door. He was with me when the police came to tell me about Jon's death. Quentin didn't act surprised. Almost like he expected it to happen. Then he asked if he could go through Jon's possessions when I got them back from the police."

Derrick perked up. "Odd and highly suspicious."

"After my attack, I asked him about the log. He said he doesn't know what it was for, but I got the feeling that he knew something about it."

"Did you tell the police about this?" Dani asked.

"Yes. They seemed to blow it off, though, like everything else I told them." Gina shook her head. "And I don't think they questioned Quentin. If they had, he would've been hurt that I suspected him, and I'm sure I would've seen it in his or his wife, Val's, demeanor."

"Sounds like we'll need to talk to him." Derrick looked at Dani. "We'll also need to get police records for their investigation into Gina's attack."

"If they even investigated." Gina felt tears prick at the memory of the night. "I'd have stayed around to follow up on them, but I couldn't risk Sophia's life. I had to get out of town."

"And so you came here, but he followed you." Derrick's gaze softened into a tender look. She'd been on the receiving end of his concern so many times that it made her heart ache to think about all she'd given up when she'd left him. "Good thing I was nearby."

"I called your agency before I booked my flight here to be sure you weren't out of town. After I arrived today, I stopped by the office, but your receptionist said you'd all left for a family event and you'd be in tomorrow. I planned to come back, but this happened tonight and so…"

"You called my cell," he finished for her.

"Please don't tell me our new receptionist gave you his cell number." Dani crossed her arms. "I've trained her on the importance of information security."

"I got it from Zach Miller," Gina said, mentioning their mutual college friend. "We've kept in contact and he's mentioned both your names recently, so I called him and he had the number."

Derrick and Dani glanced at each other, and Gina worried they were upset with Zach.

"Don't get mad at him for telling me, or for not warning you that I was in Portland," Gina said quickly. "I told him how afraid I was this man would kill me and made him promise not to tell you I was in town. I thought after our past you might refuse to see me. Under the circumstances, I'm sure you would've done the same thing Zach did."

Derrick didn't speak, but a pensive expression claimed his face.

"What I want to know," Dani said, tilting her head, "is what does Lilly's death have to do with this, and how would killing her help this guy?"

"I don't know," Gina admitted. "At first I thought he was hoping to exchange her for me, but when he killed her…" She shrugged. "We kind of look alike and it was dark in the house, so maybe he mistook her for me. Then when he got inside he realized his mistake, but Lilly had seen him by then. He could have been worried she could identify him."

"What about you?" Dani asked. "Can you ID him from the attack?"

Gina shook her head. "He wore a mask last night, but when I saw him tonight he wasn't wearing one."

"Odd," Dani said. "Were there signs of a struggle on the boat?"

Gina nodded.

"Then your friend could've tried to get away and jerked off his mask in the scuffle. Once she saw him, he had to keep her from talking."

"Or…" Derrick's eyes darkened "…he wanted you to know that he'd hurt the people around you and keep on hurting them until you surrender to him."

"So that means he'll keep coming after me. I need to leave town again. I…" Panic rose up her throat and choked off her words. She swallowed hard. "I'll have to do a better job of disappearing this time. I don't have any connections to Portland, and he still tracked me here."

"Did you use your credit card or phone?" Dani asked.

"Yes. I had to call into work and needed to pay for my plane ticket and the cab fare to Lilly's house."

"Plane tickets and cab fares can be tracked through credit card receipts," Dani said absently. "Though he'd have to possess computer skills to do so. And, of course, he'd have to get the cab company to reveal the address where the driver dropped you."

Derrick ground his teeth together. "If he found Gina using her cards or phone, the man knows what he's doing. We need to implement preventative measures. Starting right now, don't use your phone or credit card again."

How was she going to live without any money? "I don't have much cash left."

"We'll help with that," Dani offered. "I'm sure once our family hears about your situation, they'll agree to take on your case. The Justice Agency often helps people who need us but can't afford to pay."

"I can pay you. I put Jon's insurance money in a college fund for Sophia, but if you can wait until the account matures, I'll withdraw the money."

Derrick's mouth turned down. "We won't take your money."

"But—"

He fisted his hands. "No *buts*. We once meant

something to each other, and I won't let you pay for my help."

With the stubborn set of his shoulders and scowl on his face, Gina knew better than to argue. But there was no way she would take charity from a man she'd hurt so badly. Once they apprehended her attacker and solved Jon's murder, she'd find a way to reimburse Derrick before she walked out of his life for good.

Sophia fell asleep with her thumb in her mouth, and Gina laid her on the sofa while Derrick watched her tender care of the child. His desire for a family of his own spiked.

What had he been thinking when he'd insisted on taking Gina's case?

Sure, he lived for helping people in distress. He'd even trained for it with his criminal justice degree. Losing both of his parents to a car crash when he was eleven and the driver getting off with a minor punishment gave him the ability to relate. An ability that deepened further when his adoptive parents were killed, and he and his siblings founded the Justice Agency. He's always been passionate about preventing others from suffering his losses and feeling his pain.

But help Gina? She was the woman he'd loved. The woman who still stirred his interest despite their rough breakup. He'd faced murderers with ease, but how did he handle this? How was he supposed to act around her and keep his interest in check?

Especially when he saw the warmth and love on her face when she looked at Sophia. She tucked her legs up under her on the sofa and buried her chin in the collar of his old flannel shirt. He'd often found her in a similar position on cold nights in college.

"Done," Dani announced as she came back into the room.

"You got a hold of all the siblings that quickly?" Derrick asked.

She nodded.

"Are they on board with helping?" Gina asked, hope alive in her voice.

"Sorry." Dani shoved her phone into her pocket. "But they insisted on coming over to talk to both of you before deciding. They're on their way."

"Here?" Gina dropped her feet to the floor. "Tonight?"

Dani arched an eyebrow. "Is that a problem?"

"No…I…I guess not."

A knock sounded on the door, and Derrick's hand automatically dropped to his gun. "None of them could've gotten here so fast."

Dani drew her weapon and stepped in front of Gina. "I've got them covered."

Derrick eased up to the door and looked through the peephole. He blew out a pent-up breath and unlocked the door. "It's Mitch."

"This can't be good," Gina said as she came to her feet and stood next to Dani.

Derrick opened the door, but concern for Gina kept his focus on her. She stood the same height and was as regally gorgeous as Dani, but that's where their similarities ended. Gina's dark hair with red highlights caught the lamplight and contrasted with the pure yellow of Dani's. Plus Gina's nose was wider and her lips fuller than Dani's.

*Perfect for kissing.* The thought came unbidden as he remembered the kiss at the mall.

*Get a grip, Justice. Think of anything but that.*

He looked around the room, seeking a distraction from his thoughts. He had a trip planned to the Rogue River in a week, and his mouth was watering for the taste of fresh salmon.

*Yeah, that's it.* Whenever she got to him, he'd think about fishing.

Mitch punched Derrick playfully in the arm. "You lost in space, bro?"

"Do you have an update for us?" Derrick asked, avoiding Mitch's question and closing the door.

"That and questions for Ms. Evans." Mitch strode into the room with his usual take-charge attitude.

Dani gave Mitch a quick hug. "You'll be happy to know Kat's on her way here, too."

He flashed a quick smile. "Unfortunately, I'll likely be back at the scene before she gets here." His professional mask back in place, he thrust out his hand to Gina. "Ms. Evans. I'm Detective Mitch Elliot."

"Please call me Gina." She released his hand, clamped hers behind her back and planted her feet wider.

She'd always stood at attention for bad news or criticism in college. Came from years of standing up to her father. She thought it made her look tough, but he knew she was at her most vulnerable right now, tugging hard at his emotions already raw from seeing her again.

*Salmon. Steelhead. Trout. All waiting for me.*

"Please sit." Mitch gestured at the sofa and Gina complied. "I've had a chance to look at the alleged homicide scene."

"You said 'alleged.'" Gina stared at Mitch. "Does that mean you haven't found Lilly?"

"I'm sorry, but no, we haven't. Not yet." Mitch sat on the arm of a chair. "We did find signs of a struggle at the house, and I have few questions for you."

Gina flashed a worried look at Derrick.

Despite his resolve to stay aloof, a protective feeling washed over him again. He wanted to take her hand and comfort her. He should simply leave Gina's case to his family and bow out before the feeling grew into something more, but that wasn't an option. No matter the emotional toll being with her took on him, he wasn't leaving her care to anyone else. Not even his well-trained siblings.

# FOUR

Gina heard Mitch greet Ethan Justice on his way out. Mitch was returning to Lilly's boat to supervise evidence collection. He'd asked her to recount her harrowing nightmare and had asked for clarification on a few points, but overall, the questioning had gone better than she'd hoped. She believed it was in part due to his standing in the Justice family. True, Mitch was a member by marriage, but she could see he was loved and respected and that he returned their respect by treating her kindly.

Ethan, Derrick's oldest adopted brother, shuffled into the house carrying a car seat and a large shopping bag with stuffed animals peeking over the top. "Where do you want all of this, Dani?"

"By the stairs is fine." Dani took the bag from his hands and faced Gina. "I arranged for items that Sophia might need tonight."

Gina stared openmouthed as Cole followed behind, the second Justice brother loaded down with more items.

"You didn't buy all of this, did you?" she asked.

"No. Ethan bought it for his son," Dani answered. "A big, strapping baby boy like his daddy. His name's Bobby, and he's three months old."

"That's great," Gina said sincerely. Back when she and Derrick had been dating, she'd always liked Ethan. "I love that he's named after your father."

Sadness darkened Dani's eyes, and Gina felt bad about bringing up the loss of their adoptive father, who was killed along with his wife in a home invasion.

Dani set the bag on the floor and appraised Gina. "I'm surprised you remembered his name."

"Trust me. I haven't forgotten a thing." Gina's words slipped out before she thought about how Derrick would take her answer. She glanced at him in the kitchen to see if he was listening, but if he'd heard, he didn't let on.

"That's everything." Still exuding calm and focus that Gina associated with Ethan, he stepped over to her and stuck out his hand. "I'm Ethan, in case you'd forgotten."

She shook his hand. "I appreciate your kindness, but don't you need these things for Bobby?"

"Don't judge us—" he shoved his hands in his pocket as a flush crept up his neck "—but with this being our first child, we went a little overboard."

"Ha! A little?" Cole joined them. "You could care for all of the babies in a third world country with the stuff you bought."

Ethan frowned. "Suffice it to say we've got two of a lot of things."

"Then thank you for your generosity," Gina said earnestly. "I'll take good care of it until we're free to go back to San Diego."

Cole offered his hand next. His handshake was quick and firm, his face displaying no emotion as he gave his name.

A man of few words, this was so typical for him that Gina didn't take offense. "Nice to see you again, Cole."

The front door opened and a tall, broad-shouldered man as good-looking as the Justice men stepped into the room. Gina didn't recognize him, but the others clearly did.

"Luke." Dani rushed across the room. "You didn't say you were coming over."

"Self-preservation. If I wasn't here to speed things along, you'd never get home." He grinned and pulled her into his arms.

Cole rolled his eyes. "Dani's husband, in case you didn't catch that."

Luke kept one arm around Dani and smiled at Gina. "Luke Baldwin."

"Nice to meet you, Luke."

Gina wasn't surprised that Ethan, Kat and Dani had married. All of the Justices were interesting, caring people. She glanced at Cole's finger and spotted a wedding ring, too.

"So everyone but Derrick is married now," Gina said before thinking it through.

Dani looked at her twin. "And it'll be a million years before that happens. He'd have to quit making up reasons to break up with a woman first."

Brow furrowed, Derrick joined them. "Kat will be here any minute," he said, referring to Mitch's wife, the last Justice sibling, "so let's finish taking care of the baby stuff and get seated."

Dani looked at Luke. "Would you be a sweetie and carry the crib to one of Derrick's spare rooms? That way Gina can put Sophia down before our discussion gets loud and wakes her up."

"Anything for you, sweetheart," Luke said with a smile.

Dani grinned back at him and seemed to get lost in his eyes.

Derrick faked a prolonged gag, but Gina felt a pang of jealousy at Dani's happiness. A happiness that had always been out of Gina's reach.

Luke grabbed the crib. "Follow me, Gina."

"You'll want a baby monitor to keep tabs on her, too." Ethan rifled through the large shopping bag as Gina picked up Sophia. She took the monitor and followed Luke up the stairs.

Thankfully, Sophia didn't wake when Gina settled her into the crib and set up the monitor. After one last look at the little sweetheart, Gina tiptoed out of the room. She approached the stairs and heard Kat greet the others.

Gina tensed. Of all the siblings, Kat had been the most vocal in her condemnation when Gina had broken off with Derrick. A warm welcome was the last thing Gina expected. Kat had always been the defender of the family, watching to make sure no one messed with her siblings' emotions.

Gina steeled herself and marched down the stairs. Kat looked up, her eyes following Gina down the stairs. Gina forced herself to relax. She wouldn't let Kat's attitude deter her from offering a friendly greeting.

"Thank you for coming, Kat." Gina smiled and set the monitor on a table by the sofa.

Kat nodded, but it was clipped. "Let's get down to business. The sooner we figure out what's happening, the sooner you can go back to your old life." *And get out of ours* was the unspoken subtext.

"So grab a seat, everyone, and we'll get started," Derrick said cheerfully, but the look he gave Kat didn't reflect his tone.

Gina expected coming back into the Justices' lives would be fraught with turmoil. But actually experiencing it? That was more difficult than she'd thought. Maybe she really would be better off finding someone else to help her.

When all of them had taken a seat, she ran her gaze over the group. "I'm guessing my past with Derrick is the reason you decided to stop by instead of simply taking the case. Maybe it would be better if I found someone else to investigate and protect us."

"No!" Derrick shouted.

His family members stared openmouthed at him.

"I mean, no," he said calmly while peering at Gina. "We're the best investigators you can find. Plus you'd lose valuable time by looking for someone else." His eyes radiated passion and pride in his work.

He really was the man she'd once fallen in love with. A man who put helping others ahead of his own personal strife. The kind of man who would put her first at all times. The kind she fell for and fell hard.

*But he'll disappoint you again,* she reminded herself. *Just like Ben.* Men always lead you on then disappoint.

He came to his feet and surveyed his family, his focus lingering on Kat. "Anyone have a problem with taking this case, speak up now."

When no one said a word, Gina decided to acknowledge the elephant in the room. "I appreciate your help, especially with how I treated Derrick in college. I can only say I was young and thoughtless. I was trying to protect myself, but I could have—should have—found a way to do so without hurting him like that. If I could have a do-over, I would handle it much differently."

Everyone except Kat visibly relaxed a notch.

Fussy baby sounds came over the monitor, and Gina said, "I hate to keep you here longer than necessary, but would you mind if I check on Sophia? After everything that's happened in our lives lately, I'm a bit paranoid about her safety."

"Go ahead," Ethan said. "If my wife and I'd been through what you've experienced, we'd do the same thing."

"Thank you." She climbed the stairs and felt all eyes on her, but she resisted looking back. She didn't need to hear their conversation to know what they were saying to Derrick. She hurt you, they'd say. Why are you so adamant about helping her? She doesn't deserve it. Let her find someone else like she suggested.

At least that's what she'd be telling a sibling of hers in a similar situation. More than ever, she was thankful God provided people like the Justices with skills to protect her and find Jon's killer. She could only hope they would be able to look beyond her faults and work together to keep her alive.

Derrick preempted his family's questions by updating them on the case—including Mitch's involvement. When he'd finished, he sat in his favorite leather chair, planted his hands on his knees and waited for the first comment.

"With the investigation into her friend's disappearance just beginning, you must have considered she could be the killer," Kat said, sounding less than pleased.

Before Derrick could answer, Cole's focus zeroed in on him. "Do you think she's telling the truth?"

Though Derrick had waffled at first, he believed Gina's story. He nodded.

"I believe her, too," Dani said. "And if we're going to work with her, it's time for us to leave the past behind."

Derrick eyed his twin. She'd changed since she was nearly murdered last year. This willingness to easily forget about someone who'd wronged him was proof of her new approach to life—to only stress over the important things.

"Then that's good enough for me." Cole leaned back and propped a leg on his knee. "You can count on my support."

"Really?" Kat raised an eyebrow. "Just like that. Mr. Skeptical is taking her word for it?" She swung her gaze to Dani. "And you want to forget what she did to Derrick?"

Cole shrugged. "What can I say? After meeting and marrying Alyssa, I'm a changed man."

"Love will do that for you." Dani leaned her head on Luke's shoulder, and he pulled her closer.

*Right.* If only change could be that simple, Derrick would be married by now.

*Change wasn't simple for Cole.* The thought popped into Derrick's head. *Cole had tough issues— real issues from Afghanistan—to work out. If he freed himself from his problems, so can you.*

Doubt immediately set in. Cole knew his issues and could face them directly. Derrick wasn't even sure why he couldn't commit to a long-term relationship or where he'd start to fix it.

Gina came down the stairs, her focus zooming in

on him. She was seeking comfort again, and his passion for helping the underdog screamed out for him to take her hand and offer it.

*A boneheaded move.*

He shifted his focus back to the case. "I brought everyone up to speed. We're ready to make a game plan to find Jon's killer and protect you."

Kat's eyes lasered in on Gina as she took a seat. "Don't think because we're taking your case that we've forgotten how much you hurt Derrick."

"Kat fails to remember we're all grown-ups," Derrick said, hoping to take the added stress out of the room. "She still thinks she needs to protect all of us."

Kat crossed her arms. "Someone in the family has to do it."

"Since you're appointing yourself as our guardian," Dani said with a smirk, "maybe you should partner with Derrick on Gina's protective detail."

"Be glad to," Kat answered, clearly surprising Dani.

"Protective detail?" Gina's hand flew to her chest.

Derrick nodded. "One of us will be with you 24/7 until this is resolved."

"It will mostly be Derrick, but we'll all help," Dani added.

"Oh," Gina said, and quickly looked away.

*Great.* Gina's unwillingness to look him in the eye said she didn't want him around. That was bad enough, but he didn't want the sibling most likely to antagonize Gina working the investigation with him, either. He had enough drama with Gina. He didn't need Kat's, as well.

"I'll expect your full focus, and you'll have to back-burner all of your other cases," he warned.

"Ethan can reschedule the important things. Right?" She pressed her lips together and watched Ethan.

He nodded. "If that's what you want."

"It's what I want," she answered decisively and looked at Gina with a pinched expression.

Gina picked at her fingers, a sure sign she was nervous, but the smile she gave Kat didn't reflect it. "Thank you for offering. I appreciate your help and dedication."

Kat scowled and tightened her arms. Derrick tamped down a smile over how well Gina was managing Kat.

"Can we get to the plans for the investigation so I can get Dani home?" Luke asked.

Dani smiled at her husband. "I'd say finding the elusive log is our obvious first step."

Ethan looked at Gina. "Derrick told us about Jon's buddy Quentin. Can you think of anyone else who might know about the log?"

"No, and I'm not even sure Quentin knows anything," she answered. "Quentin and his wife are close friends, and I hate to think he could have anything to do with Jon's death."

"You said he lives next door to you," Derrick stated. "Was he home last night before you were attacked?"

"Yes. In fact, before the attacker broke in, when I turned off the lights to go to bed, I saw him standing outside."

"What about size and build of your attacker?" Dani asked. "Is Quentin of a similar build?"

"Yes," she agreed, but her tone lacked any conviction. "The attacker disguised his voice, so I suppose it could've been Quentin."

"Right size and build." Cole dropped his foot to the floor with a thump that shook the boat. "Acting suspicious. Disguising his voice as if you'd know him."

"So you think we're looking for someone she knows?" Ethan asked.

Cole shrugged. "It's not unheard of for an attacker who's familiar with police procedure to disguise their voice to avoid being picked out of a voice lineup."

"Voice lineup?" Gina asked. "I've never heard of such a thing."

"It's just like a visual lineup of suspects but the police have the suspect and a few other men speak, in hopes that the victim can identify the voice."

Gina shuddered. "Will I have to participate in one of those?"

"You might," Derrick said, hating to see her fearful expression. "But it may not be necessary if we can gather sufficient evidence as we work the investigation."

"It sounds like interviewing Quentin should be our first priority," Kat suggested.

Gina's eyes narrowed. "But why would he want to kill Jon? Or me, for that matter?"

"Money is always a good motive for murder," Derrick offered. "Has Quentin engaged in any lavish spending lately?"

Gina's eyes widened. "He bought a very expensive speedboat last month. That's not something he could afford on his Coast Guard salary."

"Motive," Derrick said, putting force in his word for emphasis. "We're definitely talking to him ASAP."

"You can do that while I focus on finding the log." Dani leaned forward, letting Luke's arm fall behind her. "Since Gina saw a digital photo of a log, it's likely the file was transmitted to Jon electronically."

"Unless, of course, he took a picture of the log and sent it to himself," Kat said.

"Why would he do that?" Gina asked.

Kat shrugged. "Maybe he didn't want to take the log on board his ship. Or maybe he was worried the actual log would be destroyed."

"Though those are good possibilities," Dani said, "I think I should still try to track it electronically, too."

"Agreed," Derrick jumped in. "So how would he have received an electronic copy?"

"Through email. Or a text maybe," Dani said and Derrick could almost see the wheels turning in her head. "He could also have copied it from someone else's computer or downloaded it on the internet. If

I'm lucky, I'll find a cybertrail. If Quentin's involved, it could lead straight to him."

Cole's eyes glassed over at the mention of technology, and Derrick was surprised his were the only ones. "If anyone can track down an electronic lead, it's you."

"Usually I'd be the first to agree with you," Dani replied with no modesty in her voice. "But Jon likely had a military email address. If he received the log at that account, I won't be able to access it without hacking into the Coast Guard's database, which—"

"You could do that?" Gina interrupted.

A wily smile crept across his twin's lips. "I'm sure I could, but I won't."

"Still," Cole said, "I can tell you're chomping at the bit to get your fingers on the files."

Smiling, she nodded. "I'll start on it the minute I get home tonight."

Derrick nodded. "Gina mentioned the San Diego detectives didn't believe she'd been attacked, so I'm thinking they didn't thoroughly process the scene. And with the backlog at most labs, I don't think we can count on the detective to request priority processing for any evidence they did collect."

"Sounds like a trip to San Diego is in order to question Quentin and gather evidence ourselves," Kat said.

Derrick looked at Gina. "We'll hire a private lab to run the tests and get the results in a matter of days."

She sighed. "This is all so complicated. I'm so thankful all of you understand it."

Luke looped his arm over Dani's shoulder. "Not only do they understand it, but for some odd reason, it's also what they live to do."

Dani punched his knee. "I don't knock your SEAL days, so don't knock our law enforcement background."

He saluted. "Yes, ma'am."

The family laughed, but excitement at moving forward in the case had Derrick ignoring them. "So we're agreed that Gina and I will travel to San Diego?"

Kat made eye contact. "I'll go with you."

"Of course. I'm glad to have help in protecting Gina," Derrick said. "Before we go, we should discuss backtracking Jon's and Quentin's movements. If we can see where they'd been in the weeks before Jon's death, it might give us a lead on how and where the log was transmitted."

Ethan yawned and stretched his arms overhead. "I can dig into their cell phone and credit card bills first thing tomorrow."

"Would be good if you got Quentin's full financial picture to see if he needs money or if he's received a large sum recently," Derrick added.

Ethan nodded as another yawn escaped.

"Kat, can you call in favors from your Portland P.D. buds to get the official report for Jon's accident?"

Derrick faced Gina. "Kat's a former Portland police officer and she still has contacts on the force."

"Glad to."

"Has anyone thought about this being related to the Coast Guard?" Dani asked. "Jon dealt with apprehending drug dealers on a daily basis. One of them could've wanted revenge."

Gina's eyes widened, and Derrick held up his hand to stem her concern. "That's not something we need to worry about yet, but it's an angle worth investigating."

"I still have military connections," Cole offered. "Let me see what I can dig up about Jon's and Quentin's military careers."

Ethan yawned again. "Sounds like a good start."

"Tired, old man?" Derrick teased.

"You try getting up with a baby every night and see if you're not tired, too."

"Bobby's not sleeping through the night yet?" Gina asked.

"Not all the time."

Gina launched into her past struggle to get Sophia on a regular schedule. For the first time since reconnecting with Gina, Derrick realized how tough being a single parent must be.

"Not that I don't find the baby talk fascinating," Luke said with a smirk, "but I'd like to take my wife home. So are we done here?"

Derrick nodded. "I'll make San Diego flight arrangements for Kat, Gina and me. Hopefully I can get us on the first flight tomorrow. I'll text everyone the time to be here to assist in her transport."

"Which means, with your schedule obsession, everyone can arrive fifteen minutes later," Kat said as she stood.

Derrick cast an irritated look at her. "Please don't."

"Lighten up. I was just kidding." She squeezed his shoulder. "I'll head home to pack and then come back to spend the night here as reinforcement."

It was a logical decision to have both of them on hand at all times, but Derrick picked up on Kat's hidden motive. She didn't trust Derrick not to succumb to Gina's charms tonight. Despite Kat's heavy-handed approach, he didn't mind having someone to run interference. "Then we're good to go. We'll keep in touch from San Diego by a daily video conference call unless anyone has urgent news to report."

"Let's get going before he changes his mind." Luke tugged Dani to her feet.

"Night, all." She headed for the door.

As Gina continued discussing babies with Ethan, Derrick watched Dani and Luke depart. He was glad Luke was a stand-up guy, and he wanted his sister to be happy. Really he did. But he missed the close relationship he'd had with her. Not a very manly thing to admit. But, come on. You go through life connected in a way no one can match, and suddenly that connection no longer matters compared with the new man in her life?

*Or maybe you're just miffed that you don't have*

*someone special in your life like everyone else in the family.*

Was that why he'd been irritated for months? Not because they'd moved away from him, but because he couldn't move forward himself? If only he knew how to change. He certainly didn't want to let it continue to eat at him and make him miserable, but what other choice did he have?

He needed either to get over his commitment issues or stop wanting a wife and family. He didn't have a clue how to accomplish either one. He'd have to be careful not to let his frustration over it distract him while he was in charge of keeping Gina safe.

# FIVE

Gina woke to the sun streaming in her bedroom window. She glanced around the room decorated in dark colors and contemporary furniture. A manly room.

*Derrick.*

Last night's events came crashing back. The gunshot then Lilly falling into the water. The man chasing her, his feet pounding behind as she fled for her life, sheer terror sending her heart beating faster. Then her heart heading into a tailspin at Derrick's kiss when he rescued her and Sophia.

*Sophia.*

Surprised the baby hadn't woken her, Gina listened for sounds from the adjoining room. Not a peep. She glanced at the clock. *Too late.* Had something happened to Sophia?

Gina jumped out of bed, ignoring the way her muscles ached from last night's race away from her assailant. She quickly climbed into her soiled jeans and T-shirt that had dried overnight before hurrying into the hallway.

Derrick's voice and Sophia's giggle drifted up the stairway. Gina tiptoed toward the balcony overlooking the family room. When she spotted Derrick playing with Sophia, her mouth fell open. Last night he'd made it clear that he didn't know a thing about babies. She'd assumed that he didn't want to learn—a logical extension of his commitment problem. The last thing she'd have thought he would embrace would be the responsibility for a child.

He suddenly tumbled from the sofa. Worried, Gina took a step forward, but he landed on his back and gently whisked Sophia high into the air. She squealed with delight. He settled her on his chest, and she pushed up on her elbows. They studied each other for a moment before Sophia grabbed his nose.

His joyful laugh rang through the rafters, a sound Gina once couldn't get enough of.

"You're all right, little bug, you know that?" He tweaked her nose, too. "Don't know what I was so afraid of. You aren't *that* fragile."

Sophia spouted gibberish, and he laughed again.

He'd always been lighthearted and fun loving, not the brooding man she'd encountered last night. After their relationship ended, she'd scolded herself for not seeing the warning signs that he was too carefree to want to settle down.

*And despite all of that, you're attracted to him.*

So what? With his good looks, what woman wouldn't be? But was it more than simply finding him good looking?

*Doesn't matter.* After Dani's comment last night about Derrick never marrying, it would be a mistake to follow these feelings. Plus after Ben's rejection, considering a relationship with anyone was even more foolish. She had not only her own feelings to protect this time, but Sophia's, as well.

Resolved to keep her emotions in check, she marched down the stairs to make sure Sophia had been fed and changed. "I hope she didn't wake you."

Derrick looked up at her, his smile falling. "I was already up when I heard her." He tucked Sophia under his arm like a football and, in one smooth move, came to his feet. "I thought after everything that's happened in the past few days you might want to sleep in, so Kat and I took care of her."

His kindness threatened to make tears fall. Obviously, she was still emotional from her attack. She desperately needed a good cry, but she also needed to stay strong for Sophia, and a crying jag would take her down the wrong path.

"Thank you for your help, but I can take her now." She held out her hands.

Sophia didn't extend her arms as she always did for Gina, but laid her head on Derrick's shoulder. His eyes flashed open then a wave of satisfaction flooded them. "As you can see, we've kind of become buddies."

Gina's heart melted again, but she instantly chastised herself. She didn't need a buddy for Sophia. What she needed was a guy to step up and be a strong father. A man she could count on in a relationship. But her experience said they didn't exist.

*What about the other Justice men and Kat and Dani's husbands?*

That was different. *They* were different. Trusting. They could have a meaningful relationship. She couldn't. It required her to lean on a man. To trust him. She'd tried it three times. Her father, Derrick and Ben. All ended badly. She wouldn't trust a man again. Period.

She forced her mind on to Sophia.

"Has she eaten or had her diaper changed?" Her words came out sounding terse and ungrateful so she quickly added, "Not that I expect you to have done those things."

"Kat fed her." He looked at Sophia. "You're a messy eater aren't you, Bug? A very messy eater." He grinned at her and she smiled back. "Hope you don't mind if I call her Bug. She's as cute as one, so it just seemed to fit."

He would disappear from their lives as fast as he arrived and Sophia would soon forget all about him, so it didn't matter what he called her. "That's fine." Gina looked around the room. "Where's Kat now?"

"In the office on her computer." He sat on the sofa and settled Sophia on his lap. Gina couldn't believe he wasn't eager to hand her over and get ready to depart for San Diego.

She glanced at the wall clock then reached out for

Sophia. "It's almost time to leave. I need to grab a shower, pack our things and get Sophia ready to go."

"I can watch her while you do all of that."

"I don't want to impose."

"We've got a good thing going here, and I'm glad to do it." He smiled in the lopsided way that always made Gina's heart flutter. "If she needs a diaper change or her mood takes a turn for the worse, I'll come find you."

"Okay, if you're sure."

"I'm sure." He held Sophia in the air again. "We'll have a good time, won't we, Bug?"

She giggled.

"I'll hurry and be back as soon as I can."

"Relax," he said. "Enjoy having someone around to watch her for a change so you can get things done."

As Gina jogged up the stairs, his last comment kept running through her head. She'd love to get used to someone helping with Sophia. While she was with the Justices, that's exactly what she had to guard against. If she didn't, she might find herself too close to the wrong man with her heart shattered again.

On his upper deck, Derrick peered through top-of-the-line binoculars. He scanned the river, the water clear and smooth this morning, and circled around to the dock. He didn't think Gina's attacker could have learned her location, but his gut told him to take extra precautions in her transport.

He checked his watch to confirm his departure

alarm was set to keep them on schedule. A schedule he intended to keep. No matter what. He knew only too well from his parents' accident that bad things happened when people strayed from their agenda. If he'd understood that when he was eleven and hadn't wasted time explaining away his bad grades as they were on their way out the door to see his teacher, they'd still be alive.

Cole stepped outside, drawing Derrick's focus from his watch.

"I see you're planning this thing to the millisecond as usual," Cole said as he stopped next to Derrick.

"You have a problem with that?"

Cole held up his hands. "Not me, little brother. You're the one with the problem."

"So I like to be punctual. So what?"

Cole shook his head. "Liking to be punctual is one thing, but *never* straying from your timetable? That's another thing altogether."

Derrick wasn't about to get into a discussion over this when his focus needed to be on safely transporting Gina and Sophia to the airport. A job he planned to execute in the next five minutes. Assuming he didn't spot trouble with his binoculars. He lifted them to scan a final time.

"We clear?" Cole asked.

"As far as I can tell, but something just feels wrong to me."

"Only way someone is going to get to Gina is with a rifle and a steady hand."

"If Jon's killer is Coast Guard trained, he could possess sniper skills." Derrick held out the binoculars. "I'd appreciate your taking a look, too."

Cole's brows arched. "Asking for a second opinion isn't like you at all, little bro."

"Your military experience makes you a pro at this kind of recon," Derrick quickly explained.

Cole's eyebrows rose higher. "And you want someone to confirm your observations so this thing doesn't go south."

"Exactly." Derrick shoved his hands in his pockets to warm them.

Cole lifted the binoculars to his eyes and slowly scanned the area. "Never seen you this jumpy before, bro."

That's because he'd never been this jumpy. Ever.

Cole looked over the binoculars at Derrick. "She still special to you?"

Was she? He'd let go of any residual anger he'd had over her bailing on him, but the hurt wasn't as easy to push away. Did that mean she still mattered to him? He didn't know, but he had to do everything he could not to let her stake a claim to his heart again.

He'd embraced Sophia this morning, hoping if he'd lavished her with affection, he'd forget all about Gina. Problem was, it just made him wonder what it would be like to have both of them in his life. But he barely wanted to admit it to himself, much less Cole, so he shrugged off the question.

"If you're not sure, maybe you're too close to the

situation and should leave this case to the rest of us." Cole panned the other side of the house as if he didn't care, but this was just Cole's way of letting him make the right decision without any pressure.

Not that Derrick needed to come to any decision. Point-blank, Gina would stay under his care.

"I'm good," he said, but his voice lacked confidence.

"No, you're not." Cole chuckled. "But I get it. Just don't let your emotions get the best of you."

*Easier said than done.*

Cole finished his sweep and handed the binoculars back to Derrick. "We're clear. Time to move."

Derrick offered a silent prayer for everyone's safety as they traveled through his bedroom and down to the family room. Wearing Kevlar vests, his siblings milled around, a palpable excitement that preceded a mission filling the air.

Gina sat on the sofa in a similar vest, Sophia on her lap. They'd taken every precaution, including planning to wrap Sophia in a bulletproof vest of her own. They all looked ready, but Derrick wanted to make sure everyone was on the same page.

"Quick review," he announced, gaining their attention. "Cole will keep watch on the vehicle in the parking lot. Ethan and Dani in front of Gina. Kat and I'll take the rear. We move quickly and straight to the car." He looked at Gina. "No stopping for anything. Got that?"

"Got it," she said, her voice trembling.

"Keep Sophia close to you. Don't stray from any of us." His watch sounded their departure alarm. "Let's head out."

"Maybe I should put you in charge of Bobby's schedule so I'd get more sleep," Ethan said, his tone laced with humor.

Refusing to let any of them become sidetracked when Gina and Sophia's life depended on them, Derrick ignored Ethan's jab and faced Cole. "You're out the door first."

"If you don't relax, you're going to burn out." Cole clapped Derrick on the back on the way out.

"He's right, you know." Dani went to the door to wait for Cole's signal that he'd moved into position.

Derrick ignored both of them and picked up the extra vest. He met Gina in the middle of the room. She lifted Sophia from her shoulder, and Derrick slipped the vest behind the baby then wrapped and fastened it around her with a Velcro strap.

He stood back to assess his work. "That should keep her safe."

Gina settled Sophia back on her shoulder. "Sounds like you're expecting something to happen."

"Expecting?" He thought about it for a moment before answering. "*Expecting* is too strong of a word. More like thinking something could happen, and it's better to be prepared."

She shivered, and he shoved his hands in his pockets so he wouldn't reach out to her.

Dani poked her head inside. "We're good to go."

Ethan headed out first, joining Dani just outside the door. They stood parallel to the entrance, waiting for Gina to step behind them.

Derrick nodded at the door. "You're up."

Gina marched ahead with a sigh of resignation. Kat and Derrick moved into position behind her.

"Let's roll," Derrick said.

They inched forward, pivoting like a precision drill team. Derrick was hyperaware of everything around them. The water softly lapping against his boat. Birds chirping from trees on shore. The sting of the cold on his cheeks. But he saw nothing out of the ordinary.

Ethan and Dani stepped onto the gangway—and a flash of metal from the shoreline caught Derrick's eye.

"Sniper!" he yelled and grabbed Gina. He hugged her and Sophia to his chest and tumbled toward the deck. He took the brunt of the fall on his shoulder, pain slicing up his arm just as a bullet whizzed overhead and lodged in the siding of his home.

He heard his siblings draw their weapons. He rolled to his side, putting his back to the sniper and covering Gina and Sophia with his body. Sophia startled awake and blinked her big eyes at him. Adrenaline pumped through his veins, but he forced out a smile to comfort her. Gina trembled beneath him, and he slipped his free arm around her, hoping she'd take comfort knowing he had her back.

"Everyone okay?" he called out to his family.

Dani and Ethan's affirmative answers came from

the far side of the walkway where Derrick assumed they'd found cover.

Kat duckwalked over to him. "I'll cover you while you move them behind the planter."

As gently as he could, he turned Gina to face him to assess her stability and to see if she'd be able to move as directed. She seemed alert. "Give Sophia to me, and on the count of three, make a break for the wooden planter at the edge of the deck."

"I can't let go of Sophia," she said.

"Her best chance is with me. I know how to move under sniper fire, you don't. You with me?"

She released her tight grip on Sophia, and Derrick drew the infant close. He expected her to cry, but she smiled up at him as if they were playing the same rough-and-tumble game they'd enjoyed earlier.

"One. Two. Three." Derrick didn't wait for Gina to get to her feet but lurched to his. He kept his back to the sniper and made sure to move behind Gina so he could protect her with his body. He tensed, waiting for a bullet to slam into his body armor, but none came. Together, they dropped behind the planter and rested their backs against the wood.

"Okay?" he asked Gina.

She nodded, but her eyes were still wide with fear.

Kat settled next to Derrick. "You take watch, and I'll get a unit dispatched then call Mitch."

Derrick transferred Sophia to Gina then pulled his weapon and came to a squatting position. He rested the gun's barrel on the planter and risked a quick look between the dormant rosebushes. All was quiet around them, but he kept his watch vigilant as he listened to Kat's phone conversation with the Portland Police Bureau then with her husband.

"I'm fine," she said to him. "Units are on the way, and this will all be over by the time you get here."

Derrick heard Mitch say something then Kat replied, "I love you, too."

Normally Derrick would tease her about her mushy behavior in the face of danger, and she'd offer some smart retort, but right now, he was simply glad she was alive to act all love struck, so he let it go.

His phone chimed in Cole's ringtone, making Gina jump.

"It's Cole," Derrick said to her and answered.

"I saw the sun catch on the shooter's rifle so I know his location." Cole's breath came in short bursts. "I'm headed up the hill to check on it now."

"Be careful," Derrick said as he hung up.

"Cole has eyes on the shooter's location," Derrick called out to his siblings. "He's checking it out now."

"Want to wait here or try to make it back inside?" Ethan asked.

"Everyone in a secure spot?"

"Yes," Dani said.

"Then we sit tight until we get the all clear from Cole or the police arrive."

Sophia started fussing and tugging at her vest.

"It's okay, Bug," he said to her in a soothing voice.

Kat's brows rose in question. "Bug?"

"I'll tell you later," Derrick replied. "Right now our time is better served figuring out how Gina's attacker found us."

"Any chance he followed you last night?" Kat asked as police sirens wound through the air.

Could he have let the killer track them? "I didn't think so, but with the thick fog, I suppose it's possible."

She turned to Gina. "Did you use your phone?"

"No." Gina looked as if she wanted to say something else, but she clamped her mouth closed.

Knowing how feisty she'd always been, Derrick thought she wanted to tell Kat that she knew how to follow directions and Kat didn't need to check up on her. Her indignation was a good sign that meant the shock was starting to recede.

The sirens moved closer, startling Sophia. Derrick tried making a face to calm her, still her cry ramped up, and she wailed in rhythm with the sirens. Gina cuddled her close, but tears continued to pour down the baby's cheeks, sending an ache into Derrick's heart.

Her tears were his fault. He'd let the attacker get close to her again. He had to do something to make those tears stop. He worked hard to draw her attention and made a goofy face. Her crying slowed a bit, so he exaggerated the face more. Soon she was smiling as she hiccupped away her tears and ended with a big yawn.

Kat's gaze was more watchful than usual. "Looks like you've made a friend."

No one was more surprised than him at how he felt about Bug and how she seemed to feel about him. "We have an understanding," he said to play it down.

Kat kept watching him for a moment then shook her head and came to her knees. "With the officers here, we should be good to go."

Gina started to rise, and Derrick shot out a hand to stop her. "Not just yet. Let Kat check it out first."

Gina cast a questioning look at Kat.

*Great.* Gina didn't trust him anymore and needed to confirm his decision.

"He's right. You should stay down." Kat rose. "I'll go meet the officers."

Derrick watched her leave then turned to Gina, who was staring off into the distance. Sophia had settled her head on Gina's shoulder and plugged her thumb in her mouth while Gina cuddled the little girl close. A tender scene. One that made him smile until he imagined what would've happened if he hadn't seen the shooter's weapon. His smile disappeared.

He'd failed, plain and simple, and he needed to apologize. "I'm sorry that I let your attacker get this close. I won't let that happen again."

"I'm not blaming you for this," she said but didn't look at him. "You did the best you could, and I trust you completely."

*Really?* "Then why the questioning look for Kat a moment ago?"

She shrugged but didn't answer. They'd been together for less than a day, and he was already tired of the way they were dancing around each other when they'd once been so comfortable together.

With a finger under her chin, he gently turned her head. "If we're going to spend time together, we need to talk about what happened between us in college and get it out in the open. Otherwise the distraction could put all of us in danger."

"I agree." She rested her cheek on Sophia's curls, her love for the child spilling from her eyes.

A love that she'd once had for him. The thought seared his heart. Right there in the middle of his siblings, a shooter in the wind and police lights twisting into the sky, all he could think of was how it once felt to be so connected to another person that he'd wanted to spend the rest of his life with her.

*But you couldn't,* he reminded himself. *And you still can't.*

The thoughts didn't ease the ache. He dragged his mind to fly-fishing but couldn't begin to picture a salmon or his favorite bait. Not surprising. After such a life-threatening event, he could no longer distract himself from their past. It was time to talk about it. But not here. Not now. Not with officers pounding up the gangway and his family surrounding them.

"Why don't we talk on the plane," he said, hoping when the time came that she'd still think it wise to air their differences.

"We're still going to San Diego after this?"

"The shooting gives us even more reason to move forward on the case."

She shivered. "You mean before he kills me, too?"

"I won't let that happen. I promise," he said, hoping he could keep his word. "So we're good to talk on the plane?"

She nodded, but her blank stare said she was a thousand miles away and may not know what she'd agreed to.

He got to his feet to wait for the three uniformed officers and Kat to reach the deck. Ethan and Dani climbed from their locations and stowed their weapons as the officers approached. Derrick needed to join them, but even if the sniper was long gone, he wouldn't leave Gina and Sophia outside.

"Let's get you two inside, where Sophia can sleep until this is resolved." Derrick held out his hand to help Gina and the now-sleeping Sophia up.

Derrick motioned to his siblings that he'd be right back and escorted Gina inside.

"Will the police need to question me?" she asked the moment she stepped across the threshold.

"Mitch will handle everything when he arrives. With all of us as witnesses, we should be able to provide all he needs, so you can stay in here with Sophia."

She shook her head. "Keeping me out of the loop is not an option. I need to know what's going on with the case. If you don't mind, I'll put Sophia down for a nap and join you."

Another sign that she didn't trust him? Maybe.

"It's risky to leave you out in the open."

"Can the others come inside?"

"Of course."

"Thank you." She headed upstairs, where they'd left the portable crib from Ethan. Derrick waited until she disappeared from sight then joined his siblings. Mitch had arrived and was talking with the responding officers, but his gaze kept traveling to Kat as if needing to reaffirm that she was okay.

"Can we move this little powwow inside?" Derrick asked his siblings. "Gina wants to be part of the discussion, and it's not safe for her out here."

"Maybe we should hear what Cole has to say first." Ethan jerked his head at the walkway, where Cole strode toward them. He'd fisted his hands, and a stormy look darkened his face.

Derrick's gut clamped down hard. He'd have to be blind not to see Cole had bad news to share. Derrick would rather spare Gina, but he needed to respect her wish to be included. "Gina has a right to hear everything, even if it's bad news."

Ethan gestured at the door. "Then let's take this inside."

"Mitch," Kat called. "We're headed inside for Cole's update. Want to join us?"

He nodded and, after excusing himself, crossed the deck. He circled his arm around Kat's shoulders and tugged her close. "I'm glad you're all right."

"Hey," she said, laughing, "I can't let anything happen to me now that I have you to keep in line."

He wrapped both of his arms around her, his actions testament to how badly the incident had shaken him. Mitch was a private person and a consummate professional—except for when he was worried about his wife.

Derrick could understand. He was equally shaken. Maybe more so. Gina and Sophia were his responsibility, and he needed to step up his game.

As everyone filed inside, he took a moment to thank God for keeping them safe and ask for additional protection.

A bit of peace easing the ache in his stomach, he joined the family and found Gina seated on the sofa, her fingers clenched.

Her gaze ping-ponged around the family. "You all look like the end of the world is near."

Dani sat next to Gina. "We're waiting for an update on Cole's recon."

"So does his sour expression mean it won't be good news, or is this just another one of his usual looks?" A smile tried to form, but Gina's lips trembled.

"He doesn't scowl as much since he married Alyssa," Dani responded. "We like the new-and-improved Cole so much better."

"If you two are done analyzing me," he said dourly, "I'll get started on my update."

"What'd you find?" Ethan asked.

"One shell casing."

"You left the evidence where you found it, right?" Mitch's stare was piercingly direct.

"Of course," Cole answered. "I stuck a pen in the ground as a marker so you can locate it. Or…" He let his words fall off and a smirk claim his mouth. "Since we all know feds are better trained, if you need help finding it, I'll be glad to show it to you."

Though Derrick had been a cop for years, he couldn't help but smile at Cole's reference to his former training as a U.S. marshal being superior. This kind of teasing meant Cole and the others had truly accepted Mitch as part of the family.

"Funny," Mitch mumbled. "I might be a local yokel, but I'm sure I can find it."

Everyone except Gina laughed at the good-natured bantering. "I don't get why finding a bullet casing is worth an update. I mean, we all know someone took a shot at me, so that's to be expected, right?"

"It's not that I found one. It's the type of casing that makes it important." Cole shoved a hand in his hair. "If I'm right in my preliminary look, I believe our shooter used military-issue ammo, which means we could have a trained sniper on our hands. We'll have to wait for a ballistics expert to view it."

"Doesn't compute," Dani said quickly. "A sniper isn't likely to leave a casing behind."

"Not normally," Cole explained. "But this one catapulted over a ledge and lodged in a bed of mulch. He had to know we'd be coming for him and he couldn't spend time looking for it without getting caught."

Mitch stepped forward. "If we think our shooter is military, this could help us focus our search."

Derrick shook his head. "I'm not sure how much this will narrow it down. If this is related to Jon's Coast Guard work, it's not surprising that military ammo was used."

"If it helps," Gina said, "all the men on Jon's team had intensive training in marksmanship. They disabled boats all the time by shooting out their engines. The guys used to brag about the skill it takes to hit one when flying over choppy waves."

"Is Quentin one of these guys?" Derrick asked.

"He's their best shooter."

"Even more of a reason to go to San Diego. We need to talk to him as soon as possible."

"I'll rebook the tickets," Kat offered.

Derrick met her gaze. "Change airlines to throw off our shooter."

"You think he'll try this again?" Gina asked, her eyes wide again.

"Yes," Derrick answered honestly.

"And if he's a trained sniper," Dani added, "he won't stop until he's completed his mission."

# SIX

Danger lurked everywhere. Danger presented by a foe Derrick had seen only in shadows and wouldn't recognize. It could be the man in the aisle three rows ahead. Or the one giving off bad vibes as they'd waited to board the plane. That meant Derrick couldn't let his guard down. Ever. Even while winging their way to San Diego.

It also meant he had way too much nervous energy in need of an outlet. Bouncing his leg was the only option while buckled in his seat. He'd feel a little more relaxed if he was carrying, but the law didn't allow them to bring weapons on board. They'd also chosen to pack their Kevlar vests to prevent an overly zealous security guard from detaining them. His armed siblings couldn't travel through security, and that left Gina even more exposed and vulnerable after they parted ways from the other Justices.

He glanced at her out of the corner of his eye. She sat in the window seat next to him, Sophia on her lap, contentedly playing with a plastic giraffe. She seemed calmer since they'd boarded, but maybe it was just an outward show. Once upon a time, he could've read her better, but now he didn't have a clue about the emotional turmoil going on inside.

Kat reached across the aisle and clamped a hand on his knee. "If you don't calm down, you're going to scare the other passengers. They'll think you're up to no good."

"I'll relax when we're in the air."

"Ha! I'm not buying it, baby brother. You're thinking the shooter could already be on board and you're not armed."

"Well, he could be," Derrick replied while wishing his family members couldn't read each other so well.

"We took every precaution, and no one followed us to the airport."

To keep from worrying Gina, he leaned closer to Kat. "I thought the same thing last night, and look what happened this morning."

"Ah, but this situation is totally different. It was foggy last night and you didn't have any help. It's broad daylight now with the entire family on the lookout." Her focus moved to his shoulder, and she chuckled. "Don't look now, but you're being stalked by a very aggressive seven-month-old."

Derrick swiveled to find Sophia trying to squirm out of Gina's hold to get to him. He might as well put all of his nervous energy to good use and bounce her on his knee. He held out his hands. "C'mon, Bug. Let's you and me get comfortable."

Kat snorted, but Derrick ignored her and took Sophia. Gina watched him for a moment, her cute little mouth turned down in a deep frown.

She didn't want him to touch her, but did that include Sophia? "Don't you want me holding her?"

"It's not that," she said without meeting his gaze. "I just don't want her to get used to having you around when—"

"When I can't be counted on to *be* around." He finished the sentence for her.

"I don't know what you can be counted on to do now. I only know what happened in the past."

He looked at her long and hard. "Rest assured that I'll be by your side until this man is apprehended."

"I know that. I just…" She shook her head. "It really doesn't matter, does it? This is purely a business relationship between us. We're not going to get romantically involved again."

"Exactly," he said earnestly, but his heart constricted.

She leaned closer to him. "Before we erect that professional wall, I want to make sure you know how sorry I am for the way I treated you in college. I had to leave, but I could've done it in a better way."

"Who knows? If you hadn't ended things, I'd likely have broken up with you at some point."

She considered his comment for a moment. "I hadn't thought of it that way."

Sophia climbed to her feet, so he looked around

her. "What say we put our past behind us? Once and for all, forget about it and move on."

"You forgive me, then?"

"You don't need my forgiveness, but if it'll make you feel better, yes. I forgive you and I'm letting it go."

"Thank you, Derrick. Sincerely, thank you." She squeezed his forearm. "I'm so glad we got this out in the open. Now we can focus on finding Jon's killer then go our separate ways."

*Right. Just what I want,* he thought, but his gut constricted into a hard knot again.

Didn't matter how tight his stomach got. They'd made the right decision in agreeing to keep things professional between them.

Sophia grabbed his nose again. "Is my nose overly fascinating, or is she in a phase where she grabs anything in sight?"

"Not that you don't have a perfectly fine nose," Gina said with a laugh, "but she grabs anything in sight."

Sophia babbled something then grinned at him. Despite his heavy heart, he smiled back and felt himself relax. A bit. He lifted her in the air, and she squealed. "How can you resist spoiling her rotten?"

"It's hard," Gina said. "But when I'm tempted, I remember that's what grandparents are for, and my mom and dad are taking their job to heart."

He jerked his head to face her. "You reconciled with your parents?"

"Yes. Just this year."

His mouth dropped open. "Wow. I mean, wow! I never thought that would happen."

"Neither did I," she said, listening to the flight attendant's announcement that they were cleared for departure, then taking Sophia back and holding her on her lap for takeoff. "With how far apart my dad and I were on everything, I thought it was hopeless."

He looked over her shoulder at the disappearing runway and felt the plane lift off. "You've come a long way. You wouldn't even talk to him in college. What changed?"

"It started when Jon's wife died. With him deployed for such long stretches, I got a firsthand look at life as a single parent." She sighed and Derrick could feel her pain. "Don't get me wrong. I love Sophia and I'm glad to care for her, but Becki's death was so sudden. With Jon away, I had little support."

"So you decided to talk to your parents."

She shook her head. "No, I decided to go back to church."

Another jaw-dropping statement. She'd blamed her father's dedication to his congregation for his neglect, and when Derrick had known her, she hadn't set foot in a church since high school.

"Explain, please," he said.

"I have to admit it was a selfish act on my part." She raised her voice above the rumbling engines. "Besides Becki wanting Sophia to be raised in the church, I hoped to find a community of people who could be there for us if we needed them." She chuckled softly. "No one was more shocked than me when I discovered our pastor was very successful at balancing both his family and his responsibilities."

"I don't get it. How would that help you get over your dad's treatment? Didn't it make it worse?"

"Sort of. At first. But as I watched our pastor, it made me realize that my dad was just a man like any other man who had choices to make. I could finally let God off the hook and quit blaming Him for Dad's neglect. Despite my father's example, I saw that faith and family didn't have to be either/or in my life. I could have both—which meant that I could turn to God for help instead."

"And this somehow led to reconnecting with your parents?"

She nodded. "When I quit blaming God, all that was left was my anger for my dad. I decided if I wanted to heal, I was going to have to put that anger behind me and let it go. But first I had to tell him how I felt, so I went to see him."

"And what happened?"

"I didn't have to do a thing. Before I could say anything, he apologized for using his job as an excuse to avoid his family responsibilities. I guess losing Jon made him reconsider his priorities." Sophia started fussing, and Gina lifted her to her shoulder and patted her back. "He promised that he'd changed, and he asked for a second chance."

*Crazy.* "So you gave him one. Just like that. Despite how badly he hurt you."

"No. Not right away, but I did some soul-searching and prayed. After a few weeks, I realized that in addition to blaming God, I also blamed myself for Dad's lack of attention. Why wasn't I good enough? Special enough? That sort of thing. Taking some of the blame made it easier to accept the fact that Dad wasn't going to put our family first in his life. Embracing it allowed me to go on when I felt unloved."

"Wow," he said, wondering how many times she would surprise him today. "I had no idea all of that was buried inside you."

She laughed. "Me either. But once I realized it, it also hit me that I couldn't control how Dad chose to live his life. The only thing I could control was how I responded. Him asking for my forgiveness gave me the freedom to let go of his rejection and the anger I felt for him."

"And now?"

"We've come to an understanding. He really is trying to do better, especially with Sophia. Who knows, maybe over time we'll develop a strong bond. I hope so." She planted a big kiss on Sophia's chubby cheek. "For this little one's sake." She smiled serenely.

An ache settled in Derrick's chest. He wished he'd been the one to be there for her. To be the one who could make her smile this way. Actually, to be there for *any* woman long-term.

Could he take a lesson from her father? Could he change? Be the person she'd hoped he was?

She'd wanted them to get engaged, but as much as he'd loved her, he hadn't been able to follow through on it and ask for her hand in marriage. Just thinking about it at the time had felt like a noose around his neck. If he'd known why, he'd have done something about it so she wouldn't have left.

Here he was years later, with her back in his life, and he still didn't know what kept him from making that lifetime commitment.

Did it really matter? If he managed to figure out his problem, would it make any difference with her, or would she always consider him the man who couldn't commit?

As the flight attendants gathered trash before their descent into San Diego, Gina glanced at Derrick. His head rested on the seatback, and his eyes were closed. And most notably, he'd quit shaking his leg and looking at his watch. He'd always had a thing about being on time. Kind of an obsession, as if he feared something bad would happen if he was late. When they were together, he'd refused to talk about it. She was still curious about the reason behind it.

He shifted and his leg settled against hers. A spark of electricity shot through her, but she wouldn't ask him to move. She was too glad to see him relaxed to want to interrupt his peace. He'd been so tense and wary, which she supposed a killer stalking them would bring out.

The pilot announced their initial descent, and Derrick instantly became alert. His gaze met hers for a moment then he pulled his focus away, just as he had several times since she'd shared about her dad. She wanted to ask if she'd breached that professional line so soon after they'd agreed on it, but she didn't want to get into another personal discussion.

The plane sharply descended, waking Sophia. She started whimpering and tugging on her ears. As she started wailing in earnest, Gina reached for the diaper bag.

"Can I help?" Derrick asked.

"Can you get out her bottle?"

He searched under the seat and came out holding the bottle. Gina settled Sophia in her arms and Derrick plugged it in. Sophia thrashed for a few moments then latched on, and the crying soon ceased.

Derrick looked shocked. "Does she always scream like that when she's hungry?"

Gina chuckled at his expression. "Young children don't know how to clear their ears, so the sudden change in air pressure often causes pain. Sucking on a bottle helps equalize the pressure."

"I'm thankful for bottles, then."

She laughed again.

"What's so funny?"

"The look on your face. You seem more afraid of a crying baby than of the man who's after me."

"I thought I was good with this baby thing, but after that episode…" He paused and shook his head. "Maybe I should stick to my single life."

Gina nodded sagely, while her heart ached. Few men wanted an instant family—her former fiancé was a perfect example. It wasn't hard to believe Derrick felt the same way. Hiding her disappointment, Gina watched out the window until the plane touched down and taxied to the gate. When the seat belt sign dinged, she unclipped her belt and slid forward.

Derrick held up his hand. "We'll wait for all of the other passengers to deplane."

"Why?"

"You never know who tailed us onto this plane."

"That's a little overkill, isn't it?" she asked.

He scowled at her, so she looked to Kat for an answer. "Do you think we need to stay here until everyone else is gone, too?"

"Derrick's in charge, and if he says it's necessary then that's what we'll do." Kat fired a disapproving look at Gina.

Passengers spilled into the aisle, but Gina could still feel Kat staring at her. Obviously, Kat didn't think Gina should question Derrick. Maybe she shouldn't, but trusting a man who'd disappointed her before didn't come easy.

When everyone had filed past them, Derrick got up and scoped out the plane. "We're good to go. We'll head straight for baggage claim." He looked at her. "Is your car in the parking lot here?"

"Yes."

"Good. I'm sure by now your attacker has eyes on it. We'll leave it here so he doesn't know you're back and get a rental. Kat goes first, then you." He stepped back.

She grabbed the diaper bag while balancing Sophia, who was still drinking her bottle. Gina trekked behind Kat down the narrow aisle, careful not to bump Sophia's head on a seat.

At the end of the Jetway, Kat held up her hand. "Wait here. Let me check things out first."

Derrick stayed behind and didn't speak. Gina imagined that same intensity burning in his eyes that she'd witnessed since they'd reconnected. He'd do everything within his power to keep them safe. *That* she trusted.

Kat returned. "Nothing unusual, but the place is packed, so stay between us and don't stop walking unless we tell you to."

Feeling like the filling in a sandwich, Gina trailed Kat with Derrick so close behind that she could hear the distinct sound of his shoes tapping against the floor. They wove their way down the bustling concourse to baggage claim. At the carousel, a rotund man bumped into Gina, and Derrick strong-armed the guy.

"Hey," the guy said. "Chill. It was an accident."

"Ease up, Derrick." Kat put her hand on his arm, and he let the man go. He looked up to see that everyone waiting for luggage was staring at them. "Let's move somewhere a little less conspicuous." Kat led them to seats near the bathroom and gestured for Gina to be seated.

"Get it together, bro," Kat said. "If someone is looking for us, moves like that guarantee they'll find us."

"Don't lecture me. I know." Derrick clamped a hand on the back of his neck. "Why don't you go get the rental car and the luggage? I'll stay here."

"You sure you'll be okay?"

He nodded, and Kat departed.

"Derrick," Gina said and he looked at her. "Are you overreacting like Kat said, or do you think there's a good likelihood that my attacker followed us here?"

He shrugged.

"I'm a big girl, and you don't need to sugarcoat things for me." Feeling the need to prove her strength, she stood.

He fisted his hands and looked away as if her comment angered him.

She touched his arm, and he jerked around to face her. "He could be here. I don't know. That's what has me spooked. I just don't know."

"Haven't you been in situations like this before?"

"Yes."

"How did you handle them?"

"They were different," he said softly as he turned away. "I wasn't protecting you and Bug."

She hated to see him upset, but her heart thrilled to hear him say she and Sophia were different.

*Easy, Gina,* she warned herself. *Don't let thoughts like that take flight, or you'll be setting yourself up for a world of heartache.*

# SEVEN

Stifling fumes from cars idling in the airport pickup area irritated Derrick's throat as he settled Gina into the rental car. Her sweet perfume rose up to meet him, and his mind flashed back to his earlier statement. He couldn't believe he'd actually told her that he was off his game because of her and Sophia. He might as well have rented an airplane to fly overhead declaring he still had a thing for her.

Worse, her vulnerability when she spoke of her father made him want to wrap his arms around her all the more. He slammed the door, hoping it would draw his focus back to his job.

*Protect her. That's all she wants from you.* She'd made that perfectly clear after his disclosure, when she'd looked shocked and sick before dropping to the bench without a word.

"We good to go?" Kat asked, meeting his gaze. "Or is there a problem?"

"No problem." He turned and scanned the area one last time.

A few families, a high school athletic team in Kelly green tracksuits and an elderly couple milled around the doors. None of them appeared to pose a threat, so he slid behind the wheel and waited for Kat to climb in next to him.

She swiveled to face the back window. "Make a trip around the airport, and I'll watch for a tail."

Derrick heard Gina's quick intake of breath, and he wondered when she'd quit being surprised by the fact that her attacker wasn't going away.

"It'll be okay, Gina," Kat said, her tone surprisingly soft. "We'll get you through this in one piece."

Derrick maneuvered out of the pickup space and merged into the traffic inching forward. He kept a razor-sharp watch on the surroundings, but no one stood out. So what? If he were stalking someone and trying to kill them, his training would ensure he wouldn't stand out either. Nor would any of his siblings. Just like the suspect wouldn't if he was a trained sniper. That's what made this so dangerous. Their killer could blend in anywhere at any time.

Derrick followed the ramp to return to the airport and stayed in the outer lane to avoid cars in the pickup lane. Though they'd all donned Kevlar vests in the bathroom and his weapon rested securely in the console, he would stay in hyperalert mode until they cleared the hotel and Gina was safe behind a locked door.

He glanced at Kat. "Anything?"

"Maybe. Make another trip around."

"Maybe" in Kat's terms meant "likely"—she'd couched her answer not to worry Gina. Derrick moved his hand to his gun and made the return circle.

"Looks like we've got a tail." Kat drew her gun from the holster. "Black sedan. Three car lengths back. Two men in the car."

"Two," Gina exclaimed. "Now there're two men after me?"

"I can't be certain they're tailing us," Kat replied. "But my gut says I'm right."

"Then it's time for evasive maneuvers." Derrick searched the area hoping to formulate a plan.

The upcoming ramp to the freeway would do nicely.

"Get ready," he warned. "I'm going to hit the gas to cut across to the ramp. Hopefully they won't be able to react fast enough. It'll be rough, so hold on."

"Is this really necessary?" Anxiety laced Gina's words.

With the black sedan threatening, Derrick knew this action was not only necessary, but it was essential to keeping all of them alive.

He met her frightened gaze in the mirror. "We have no other option."

"Derrick knows what he's doing," Kat said. "As a cop, he was trained in high-speed driving, and he's almost as good at it as I am." Kat chuckled.

"Almost?" Gina croaked out.

"Sorry," Kat said sincerely. "You probably aren't in the mood for a joke right now."

"No."

"You might need to get used to it. Joking is what we do to relieve tension. If the past incidents are any indication, we'll likely have to crack a few jokes until we find your attacker."

Derrick glanced in the rearview mirror. "I need you to lie down on the seat, Gina."

"What? Why?"

"If my plan doesn't work, I don't want them taking a shot at you."

"But what about Sophia?"

"I've got her." Kat climbed over the seat and protected Sophia with her body. She made funny noises for Sophia, who giggled. It was the first time the sound failed to bring a smile to Derrick's face.

"Okay, here we go." He floored the gas and cranked the wheel hard, whipping his car across several lanes of traffic. Brakes squealed and horns blared, but he successfully made the change. Now he had to negotiate a sharp curve ahead, and then hopefully they'd be home free.

He glanced in the mirror. The black sedan made the same death slide, careening off another car and sending it into the wall. They roared toward them.

"Hold on," Derrick warned. "Looks like they're going to try to ram us on the curve and run us over the embankment. I'm going to slam on my brakes and they'll hit us hard."

"No," Gina said, her face white as a sheet.

"Derrick will handle this," Kat said. "He's a pro."

Derrick started into the curve then suddenly hit the brakes. The sedan slammed into their bumper, and Derrick steered into the curve. The muscles in his arms screamed to release the wheel, but he held firm and they squealed around the bend.

Unprepared, the sedan lost control and plummeted over the embankment. A loud crash echoed up, but Derrick didn't have time to revel in his success. He had to negotiate the rest of the curve first.

"Everyone okay?" he called out as he slowed to a safe speed and glanced in the mirror.

"Fine," Kat said.

"Is Sophia okay?" Gina popped up and craned her neck around Kat.

"She's fine, aren't you, sweetie?"

Happy sounds came from Sophia.

Derrick glanced at Gina again. "I'm sorry you had to go through that after losing Jon and his wife in car crashes."

"It wasn't your fault." She gulped in a few deep breaths. "I'm just glad no one was hurt."

"See you later, little one." Kat planted a loud kiss on Sophia's cheek then climbed back over the seat.

Derrick knew he needed to lighten up the mood to help Gina settle down after yet another attempt on her life.

"Good thing you were with me instead of Dani," Derrick said to Kat. "She'd never get her long legs over the seat, but your little stubs…" He let his voice fall off and braced himself for the punch to his arm, which came as she settled in the passenger seat.

"I love you, too, little brother." Her sarcasm made him laugh.

"How about plugging the hotel's address in the GPS?" He dug out his phone and handed it to Kat. "You'll find it in my last text from Dani."

"Let's hope that her reservation tactic was enough to keep those thugs from finding us again."

"What tactic?" Gina asked.

"She booked the suite using a PayPal account instead of a credit card that could lead back to our agency," Derrick said.

Kat peered back at Gina. "And she waited until we arrived to make the reservation, so if anyone did somehow find out where we were staying, they wouldn't be sitting there waiting for us."

"There's no way they can find us, then?" Gina asked, her hopeful tone begging for confirmation.

"Not exactly," Kat answered. "Despite our best efforts, they found us at the airport."

"I don't understand. After all the precautions you took, how could they have done that?"

"That's the question of the hour," Derrick said. A question he needed to answer quickly if he was going to keep Gina alive.

Gina pressed her hand one last time on Sophia's back then tiptoed out of the hotel suite's bedroom. She found Derrick and Kat sitting at the dining table, where she'd left them thirty minutes ago. They were still discussing how her attackers had found them at the airport. It sounded like the only possible explanation they'd reached was that they'd had someone watching arrivals at the San Diego airport, and a team standing by in their car to tail them.

"Don't worry, we'll figure it out," Kat offered.

"I wish I was as certain as you," Derrick said, to Gina's surprise.

"You don't think we'll figure out how they tracked us?" Gina asked as she approached. "So that means they'll find us again."

"I didn't say that." Derrick pushed to his feet but didn't offer any reassurance. "We should get over to your place while there's still daylight."

She looked at Kat. "Are you sure you don't mind keeping an ear out for Sophia while we're gone?"

Kat held up Jon's accident report that she'd received via fax. "If she wakes up, she'll be far more interesting than this report. Besides, I might need the practice."

"You're pregnant?" Derrick's voice shot high.

"No, but not for the lack of trying."

"TMI, Kat." He plugged his ears. "TMI."

Gina remembered nothing was off-topic for Kat if it had the potential to embarrass her youngest brother, or so he claimed. He dropped his fingers, but his face had reddened. Gina chuckled over his embarrassment. He was such a study in contrasts. The big, tough guy who faced danger all the time but turned

into a marshmallow when his sister mentioned trying for a baby.

He grabbed a Kevlar vest and quickly shrugged
into it. "Put your vest on and wait here while I check
out the parking lot."

As she slipped into the vest, which was becoming standard procedure now, he checked his gun and
went outside.

She secured the Velcro tabs and settled her jacket
over it. She caught sight of herself in the mirror and
laughed at her reflection. "It looks like I've gained
ten pounds."

"Actually the vest weighs around six pounds,"
Kat answered without looking up from her file. "Six
pounds that could save your life, so keep it on."

Disappointment evaporated Gina's smile. She'd
tried to lighten up and joke with Kat, but obviously,
she was still miffed at Gina for hurting Derrick and
didn't want to joke with her.

Derrick stuck his head in the door. "We're good
to go."

Gina joined him in the hallway. Derrick had insisted on a first-floor suite with direct access to an
exit. She stepped away from him to the exterior
door, but he caught up and slid his arm around her
waist, pulling her close. His musky scent clung to
him, bringing back memories she had no business
remembering. She put a little space between them.

"Don't argue." He tightened his hold. "I want you
close to me."

She stayed put. Truth be told, she reveled in the security she felt with his arm around her. It was the other feelings she was rebelling against.

He escorted her to the car, and after he laid his gun on his lap they departed. At the first corner, he turned in the opposite direction of her home.

She looked at him. "I thought we were going to my apartment."

"We are," he replied, not taking his eyes off the road. "But I'll make a few left turns first to see if anyone is following us."

"I take it turning left is important."

He nodded, his focus now moving between mirrors. "Odds are against anyone making as many left turns in a row as I plan to make."

She shook her head. "This is all so surreal. I went from being an average citizen to someone more like a character you see fleeing in action movies. If I was on my own, I'd have no idea how to protect myself. It's a relief that you and your family are so skilled in this line of work. Makes me realize how blessed I am to know you."

He cast a wary look at her but said nothing.

"Did I say something wrong?"

"No. It's great that you recognize our skills."

"But?"

"But what?"

"There was a *but* in your voice."

He shrugged, and she could see that he'd shut down. He would no more tell her what was bothering him now than he'd explain his standoffish attitude since they'd left the airport. She gave up and watched out the window until they pulled into her apartment driveway. She handed him her parking garage keycard, and he swiped it to raise the metal bar. They wound through the lot up to the third floor, his eyes alert, checking every nook and cranny.

He parked next to the walkway leading to her apartment. "We'll cross over the same way we walked to the car. Nice and tight."

He climbed out and as she followed, he grabbed a backpack from the backseat and shrugged it over his shoulders. Uncertain how to approach him, her steps faltered. He'd caught her by surprise at the hotel when he'd slipped his arm around her, but as she moved toward him now, it felt awkward knowing he'd draw her close again. She'd once settled next to him without a thought, and the longing for that kind of ease with him made her cringe over her foolish thoughts.

He didn't seem as ill at ease as he confidently reached out, and she slipped under his arm. They took the covered walkway, each step reminding her of the attack that had taken place in her apartment and raising her apprehension. At the building entrance, a shiver traveled down her body.

He looked at her. "Hey, relax, I won't bite."

She forced a smile. "It's not you that I'm worried about."

"I know, but I thought a little humor might take

your mind off it." He slid her keycard down the electronic reader, releasing the lock.

As they shuffled together into the hallway, Derrick's touch gave her strength. In an effort to match his, she forced back her shoulders. She couldn't let her attacker intimidate her any longer. She'd always taken care of herself, and she couldn't let herself sit back and wait for Derrick to handle her every need.

She tried to slip her key into the door, but trembling hands made it difficult. He settled his hand over hers and held it steady as she turned the lock.

"Thank you." She looked up at him, his face close enough to feel his breath on her cheek.

He smiled, brightening his whole face, returning him to the youthful man who'd played practical jokes and always, always had a beaming smile for her in college. They locked gazes, and she got lost in his eyes as her pulse tripped higher.

A door slammed down the hall, and he whipped his head up and searched the area as he quickly moved her inside. He closed and locked the door, that hard mask covering his face again.

"This is why your suggestion to keep things professional is such a good idea." He shrugged out of his backpack. "No more mooning at each other out in the open like that."

She nodded, but she was disappointed at how easily he dismissed their ongoing attraction while she was still struggling.

He drew latex gloves from the pack and shoved

them into the pockets of his jeans. "Walk me through the apartment and show me the path your attacker traveled."

*Good. Focus on the attack. That's sure to get rid of any warm feelings.* "Since there was no sign of forced entry, I think he used a key to come in the front door. Where he got one, I haven't a clue."

"Could someone have duplicated your or Jon's key?"

"My keys were always with me except at school, where I lock them in my office. Jon left his at home when he was deployed. After the accident, the police had them until they returned his things to me."

"Maybe someone conned one out of your building manager. We'll talk to him before Quentin." He surveyed the room. "Where'd your attacker go after he entered?"

"Nothing was disturbed out here, so I'm assuming he wanted to talk to me before searching for the drive. If that's true, he headed straight to my room and would've come this way." She started down the hallway. "This first room is mine. Sophia's is next and Jon's is…was at the end of the hall."

"That means your attacker wouldn't have needed to go beyond your door."

"That's my take on it." She stepped into her room.

Sheets and blankets dangling from the bed brought back visions of the night. The attacker's hand going over her mouth. The gun pressed to her head. The resounding click of the trigger when he'd fired. Her mad scramble out of the covers to grab her gun from the drawer.

Panic pressed on her mind, and the room closed in. A sob climbed up her throat, but she swallowed it back and forced her shoulders into a hard line.

"I was awake but I was listening to music on my headphones, so I didn't hear him until he came into the room." Her voice came out in a whisper. She pointed at a small cardboard box on the dresser. "The flash drive he wanted was with Jon's things in that box. I got up and gave it to him. That's when he pulled his gun and cocked the…" She couldn't recount her story again. Not in the room where it happened. She turned away.

"Hey." Derrick stepped close and rested his hands on her shoulders. "It's okay."

A shiver racked her body. "It was terrifying."

Derrick slid his hands down her arms, and his touch pulled the sob out. She looked up at him, trying to focus on his eyes to calm her nerves, but tears clouded her vision.

"Shh, don't cry." He gently drew her to his chest.

She tried to keep her tears at bay, but she couldn't hold them back. She hadn't cried since the attack. Now she let them go. Freely, voraciously, she cried, clinging to his shirt and soaking it while he rubbed soft circles on her back. When she could finally breathe again, she leaned back and peered at him.

"Sorry." She pressed her hands against his solid chest to put distance between them.

He held fast with one arm and swiped a tear from her cheek with his thumb. "No need to apologize. Is this the first time you've let yourself cry?"

She nodded.

He trailed his finger down her face and let it fall. "Feel better?"

Did she? Or did his kindness make her feel worse? She'd forgotten how wonderful it was to be with a man who could be so tender and loving. The longing that followed was the last thing she needed right now.

"I'm good." She extracted herself from his arm. Digging a tissue from her jacket pocket, she dried her eyes.

His focus never left her. "You ready to go on?"

Was she, or was she more ready to forget their agreement to keep things professional and move back into the safety of his arms?

*Not an option.*

With iron will, she nodded then walked to the other side of the room. "When his gun jammed, I grabbed mine from my nightstand and fired at him. He ran. I followed to make sure he left through the front door then I called 9-1-1."

"I know that was hard, but hearing the details will help me know where to look for evidence." He dug the gloves from his pocket and snapped them on. "I'll start by collecting a sample of the blood you mentioned. Can you show me where it is?"

Her face still burning from his touch, she rushed past him and led the way back to the family room.

Near the front door, she pointed at the bloodstains on the tile floor.

He pulled swabs and evidence bags from his pack then squatted and studied the area. "Not a lot of blood but enough to at least consider that you winged him." He took out a swab and set to work.

She felt useless—and she needed to stay busy to keep her mind off the connection that still existed between them and off the attack. "What can I do to help?"

"There's really nothing you can do while I gather the evidence. Your role comes when we talk to Quentin." He put the first swab in a bag and peered up at her. "Is there anything you need to do around here? Something not in the areas your attacker traveled."

Gina didn't have to think long about his question. "I'd love to grab a few things." She tugged on her plain black shirt. "Something a little nicer to wear and some supplies for Sophia from her room would be good. And my violin. We left with the barest minimum of things."

"You can get the things from Sophia's room, but please wait until I finish processing your room before going back there."

She wouldn't admit it to him, but she'd gladly wait to have him accompany her. She might want her favorite clothes, but she suspected it'd be a long time before stepping into her room no longer made her cringe in fear.

# EIGHT

"I found enough blood on the floor to suggest Gina winged her attacker," Derrick said over the phone to Kat. "If so, he could've sought medical attention."

"Let me guess," Kat replied. "You want me to contact all the hospitals and clinics in the area to see if a man came in with a questionable injury?"

"Yes, and I need you to get started on it immediately." Derrick put the last forensic sample into his backpack and zipped it closed then joined Gina at the dining room table.

"That means I'll have to put aside my investigation into the crash."

"Then do it," he said forcefully as the images of Gina cowering in fear in her room kept pummeling his brain. "The faster we act, the better our chance of finding the man who attacked Gina before he tries something again."

Gina tensed at his comment and Derrick felt bad, but he had to convince Kat to make his request a top priority. "Call me if you find anything before we get back to the hotel."

"Please," Kat added.

"Please," Derrick repeated as Gina leaned forward and mouthed "Sophia." Derrick nodded and said into his phone, "Gina wanted me to ask how Bug is doing."

"Gina, really?" Kat laughed. "You're obviously growing attached to Sophia. Are you sure you're not the one who's interested?"

"Kat," he warned, "this isn't the time to get into it."

"Okay," she conceded surprisingly fast for her stubborn personality.

Derrick didn't take comfort though. He knew that even though she'd let it go now, she'd bring it up again. "So about Sophia?"

"I have the monitor right next to me, and she hasn't stirred."

"I'll tell Gina." His call waiting beeped, and he looked at the screen. "I have to go. Dani's on the other line. Make sure you call if you find anything." Derrick clicked his call waiting. "Sis."

"Good, I'm glad I caught you," she said excitedly. "I've got an update on the case."

"Tell me it's good news," he demanded as Gina watched him carefully.

"Could be," Dani replied. "I've got Ethan and Cole with me. I just need to add you and Kat for a quick video call."

"No can do. Kat's at the hotel, and I'm with Gina at her apartment."

"And how are things going with you and Gina?"

Wondering the same thing, he looked at Gina. "About as well as can be expected."

"Ah, I get it. Gina's right there and you don't want to elaborate, but I can hear the tension in your voice."

"What did you expect?"

"I don't know," she said, sounding surprised. "For years, I was really miffed at her for taking off on you, but after nearly dying last year, most things that bothered me just don't seem so important anymore." She paused. "I'd be glad to threaten your life if you think it'll help you the same way." She laughed.

He groaned. "Time for the call."

"Then I'll phone Kat. By the time she's logged on, you should be ready, too."

Gina watched him warily. "Good news?"

"Dani thinks it could be. Either way, it's important enough to get our entire family on a video call." He dug his tablet computer from the backpack. "I'll set up the screen between us so you can participate in the call, too."

He set his computer on the table then straddled a chair and clicked on the video settings. As the little button on the screen whirred, indicating the computer was connecting to his wireless provider, he glanced at Gina.

She'd twined her fingers together, settled them on her lap and now was staring at them. She'd been through so much in the past few months. Losing Becki and Jon. Becoming a full-time mother. And now a creep was trying to kill her. Took a strong woman not to completely fall apart under that kind of stress. But then, the way her father had ignored her while she was growing up had made her strong and independent. Just like God said when He promised to bring good things from bad.

*How about manning up and seeing how He's doing that for your good, too? Maybe find a way around your problems.*

"Ready, guys?" Dani's voice suddenly came over his computer.

He focused on the screen, which was divided into sections. Dani's face filled a large center box and the other siblings peered from smaller boxes surrounding her. He turned the computer so both he and Gina could see the screen. "Go ahead, Dani."

Gina sat forward. "Before you start, I'd like to ask if anyone has an update on Lilly."

Kat shook her head. "I talked to Mitch a few minutes ago. They're still looking for her."

"Any leads at all?" Derrick asked.

"Only the slug recovered from the siding of your house. Until they find Lilly, he has nothing to compare with it. But you know Mitch. He won't give up until he's found her and the shooter."

"She's right, Gina," Ethan said. "Mitch is one of the best."

"One of?" Kat repeated, smiling. "He *is* the best."

Despite Kat's joking, Gina stared at her clenched hands again.

"You've made progress though, right, Dani?" Derrick asked, hoping to ease Gina's discouragement.

"I did," she said. "I accessed Jon's personal email account and found an interesting email to Quentin. It's about an off-book investigation the two of them were conducting into their teammate Perry Axton's death."

"Perry?" Gina looked up. "But the official investigation was closed a while ago."

"Maybe they recently discovered something new." A bright box glowed around Ethan's picture as he talked. "Something that got Jon killed. Gina, can you share what you know about Perry's case?"

"All I know is that he was killed in a drug raid about six months ago. The team was trying to arrest some big drug lord, and Perry got caught in the crossfire."

"You said the case was closed." Cole's deep voice boomed through the speakers. "Who investigated his death?"

"I can answer that," Dani announced, preempting Gina. "I did a little research before I called. The San Diego Police Department and the Coast Guard both investigated the case."

"So if the SPD was involved, that means Perry died in the area." Derrick pondered how this case might be related to Jon's death. "Anyone prosecuted for the murder?"

Dani shook her head. "Not that I can see, but I

wanted to get this information to you before digging any deeper."

"Here's a crazy thought," Ethan jumped in. "What if Perry was killed by friendly fire? Maybe Quentin was the shooter. He covered it up. Jon found out about it and was going to report Quentin. So he ran Jon off the road."

Cole frowned. "I hate to say this, but it wouldn't be the first time a soldier was killed by friendly fire and someone covered it up."

Gina shook her head. "I don't buy it. Quentin and Jon were best friends. He wouldn't kill Jon for any reason."

Derrick met her gaze. "But you think he might be the man who attacked you, and that your attacker was Jon's killer. At least you were leaning that way last night."

"I know. I just…I can't believe it, I guess." She looked so forlorn that Derrick took her hand, noting that her fingers were ice cold. He cupped them between his, and surprisingly she didn't pull away.

"Let me work my sources to see if I can get a copy of the official Coast Guard report," Cole offered.

"I'll try to get the same report from the police." The box around Kat's picture lit up. "If I can get the ballistics information, I'll ask Mitch to compare it with the slug recovered from this morning's shooting."

Derrick sat forward. "Gina and I are talking with Quentin next. Maybe I can get him to open up about Perry's death."

Cole scoffed. "Good luck with that. Getting *anyone* in the military to talk with a civilian about a mission is about as likely as getting Kat to quit meddling in our lives."

All the siblings smiled, including Kat. For a moment, at least, but then she stabbed a finger at her screen. "Mighty brave of you, Cole, to attack me while I'm not there to defend myself."

Dani swung around, and her arm flew past her web camera.

"Ouch, Dani." Cole rubbed his shoulder. "What was that for?"

She laughed. "I punched him for you, Kat, and he's crying like a baby."

Kat chuckled. "Serves him right."

Ethan rolled his eyes. "Can we focus? I'd like to get home sometime today."

"Uh-oh," Kat said. "Sounds like Bobby kept you up last night again."

Dani nodded. "He's been a real bear all day."

"Focus, people," Ethan grumbled.

"See?" Dani laughed then fell silent for a moment.

"Okay, seriously, guys—enough." Ethan cleared his throat and they sobered up. "Just a word of caution. Without any proof of the friendly fire theory, let's not embrace it at the cost of investigating other motives. I don't want us to lose sight of the fact that Quentin bought this crazy expensive boat and the motive we're looking for could still be money."

"I've been thinking about the boat," Gina said. "He could've won the lottery or gotten an inheritance."

Derrick couldn't believe she was still defending him. "More likely he got involved in drug smuggling through his job."

"No!" Gina said firmly.

"I know you don't want to think a family friend is involved in the drug trade," Ethan said, "but people can disappoint us."

Gina looked straight at Derrick and he assumed she was thinking of his inability to commit to her.

"Hey," Dani said, "let's not come to blows over this. After all, it's pure speculation. Maybe I can find something in a search of Jon's computer that will help solidify one of our theories. I can walk Derrick through it when we get off the phone."

"Good luck, bro." A note of sarcasm vibrated through Ethan's voice. "You're in for an hour or more of geek speak."

"Ha-ha," Dani said quickly. "Keep laughing and good luck getting help next time you need something tech related to solve one of your cases."

Instead of the support she'd hoped for, Derrick and his siblings laughed harder, confident she wouldn't follow through on her threat.

"See what I put up with, Gina?" Dani complained. "I save them all the time when they run into dead ends, and I get no respect."

Gina's mouth opened and closed as if she didn't know how to respond to their banter. With the tense family she grew up with, she'd always been unable to lighten up when visiting his family in college.

Ethan leaned closer to his camera. "Don't worry, Gina. Dani may be a pain in the rear, but we love her just the same."

"Before this conversation deteriorates further," Dani said, "I'm kicking all but Derrick off the call. Say goodbye, everyone."

A chorus of goodbyes sounded through the computer. As the various windows closed, Derrick was struck by how much he actually missed his family and wished they were here to help with the case. He wasn't sure if it was from his worry over Gina or if the time spent with her reminded him of his dreams for a family of his own.

Dani clapped her hands, the sound resounding through Gina's apartment. "Okay, let's get started. Take me over to Jon's computer and boot it up. That is if you can figure out how to turn it on."

"Funny." Derrick grabbed his tablet and crossed to a small desk. He found the computer running and shook the mouse to wake it up.

Gina pulled a chair up to the computer. "Jon and I shared this so you'll have to use his login. It's jonw, all lowercase."

Derrick entered jonw. "Password?"

"I don't think he had one."

Derrick hit Enter, but access was denied. "He had one."

"That could mean he felt a need to hide something

and we're on the right track." Excitement gleamed from Dani's eyes. "His login is pretty basic, so I'm guessing he'd use something simple for a password. Start with 1234."

Derrick plugged it in. "Access denied."

"How about a birth date?"

"He'd likely use Sophia's." Gina rattled off the date.

Derrick entered the numbers and access was granted. "We're in."

Dani crossed her arms and stared into her screen. "Now do you understand why I lecture all of you about not using simple passwords that anyone can guess?"

"I understand why we shouldn't use obvious passwords, but the lecturing? I'll never understand that." He winked at Gina.

"Like I mentioned before, Gina," Dani said.

"You get no respect." Gina smiled, and he was thankful for his sister's ability to keep things light.

"Let's start with his browser history," Dani said.

Derrick clicked on the internet icon on Jon's desktop. He selected the option to see the entire history.

"It's empty." He turned to Gina. "Did you clear his history?"

"No," Gina said. "And at great risk to myself, I'm going to admit in front of Dani that I'm not fond of computers, and I'm not sure I know how to do it."

"Not fond of computers!" Dani cried out. "It's

a good thing I'm not there, or I might've had to hurt you."

"Don't worry." Derrick grinned at Gina. "You're already under my protection. What's one more person to save you from?"

She smiled back, but it was halfhearted, and he felt like a dope for reminding her of her attacker.

"Since the history was cleared," Dani went on, "let's move to his email."

Derrick opened the program and scanned the account. "Wiped clean. Nothing sent or received."

"Interesting." Dani tapped her finger on her chin. "Thank goodness he used an email provider with online access, or I would never have found the message from Quentin."

"So if you can access it online, what's the point of deleting the files on the computer?" Gina asked.

"It's possible he never downloaded his email, just read it online."

"Or there could be something on the computer worth hiding and our suspects broke in to delete it," Derrick said.

"Right. So if you pull the hard drive and overnight it to me, hopefully I can reconstruct the data."

"Or you could get on a plane and look at it here." Derrick directed a serious look at Dani so she could tell he wasn't joking.

She frowned. "You might be right, but I'd rather not leave my current cases. Gina's not our only client. So unless you really need me…"

"Two goons tried to end our lives at the airport, and we don't know how they found us. I'd appreciate having another pair of eyes in case they manage to find us again." He cast his best pleading look at his webcam.

Dani groaned. "Pouting will not work."

"I'm not pouting," he said innocently.

"Is he pouting, Gina?"

Gina studied him. "Yeah, and I don't know about you, but it always worked on me."

"Guilty." Dani chuckled. "I'll book the earliest flight I can and let you know when I arrive."

"Thanks, sis."

"Yes, thank you," Gina added. "I appreciate the sacrifice you're making."

"Don't worry." Dani offered an exaggerated wink. "Derrick will owe me a big favor, and I plan to collect on it."

Smiling, Derrick shut down the computer in preparation for removing the drive. He knelt on the floor to unplug the cords and caught sight again of the blood from Gina's attacker on the floor. His smile evaporated. A killer was still after Gina, and he was suddenly very glad that another capable person would soon be added to Gina's protection team.

As Gina approached Quentin's door under Derrick's watchful eye, she couldn't hide her disappointment in striking out with the building manager. He'd promised that he hadn't given a key to anyone, and he wasn't missing one, so that was a dead end. Maybe Quentin would provide a lead.

She knocked on Val and Quentin's door and heard their children running through the foyer, screaming with excitement.

"Prepare yourself," Gina said to Derrick. "They have two preschoolers who can be a handful."

"I guess it'll give me an idea of how Bug is going to change. Not that I'll get a chance to see it."

At his wistful tone, she shot a look at him. It almost sounded like he wanted more out of life than a single guy could have. But if that was the case, why wasn't he married by now?

The door suddenly opened, and Derrick's hand went to his weapon. When Gina spotted Val looking frazzled, she felt guilty that she often let one small baby tire her as much Val's energetic kids.

"Gina!" Val stepped in front of the children then dragged Gina into a hug. "I thought you'd left town."

"I did, but I'm back." Gina melted into her friend's hug while emotions simmering below the surface threatened to bring tears again. She pushed out of Val's embrace.

"Can we watch TV, Mom?" her son asked, sounding bored.

"Yes," Val answered without taking her eyes from Gina as both children scampered away. Val's gaze went to Derrick. "And who might you be?"

"Derrick Justice." He held out his hand.

Val shook hands but her focus swung to Gina. "*The* Derrick Justice? As in the one—"

"I went to college with," Gina finished for her friend and gave her a warning look. "He's a private investigator now, and he's helping me find the man who attacked me. We're hoping to talk to Quentin."

"Oh, girl, look at me." Val fluffed her hair. "Do you think I'd look this wiped out if he was here to help? He got called away yesterday and won't be back until late tonight." She shook her head. "It's bad enough that he's out to sea most of the year, but to call him out on his leave? Unfair."

"So he's on duty?" Derrick asked.

"Where else would he be?" Val asked casually then eyed Gina. "Unless you know something you're not telling me."

"Relax, sweetie." Gina rested a hand on Val's arm. "We didn't even know he was gone, so we don't have any information that you don't have."

Val blew out a breath. "I'm sorry for being such a ninny, but you know how it is living with thoughts of him getting hurt in the back of your mind all the time."

Gina nodded. She'd felt the same worry for Jon whenever he'd been deployed. Ironic, since he actually died in his own car on U.S. soil.

Derrick held out his phone. "Would you both excuse me for a minute? I just remembered a call I need to make."

Gina flashed a questioning look at him, but he didn't respond other than to move out of earshot.

Val stepped closer. "So dish. What's going on with you two?"

Gina shrugged it off. "It's purely business."

"Mmm-hmm." A knowing smile spread across Val's lips. "Just what kind of business have the two of you been up to?"

Gina tapped Val's forehead. "You can stop all those crazy thoughts racing through your mind right now. He's simply helping me find my attacker. End of story."

"Mmm-hmm," Val said again then grinned. "So where's Sophia?"

"Staying with Derrick's sister someplace safe."

Val's smile fell. "This is all so surreal, isn't it? I used to think this was a safe complex, but after your attack…"

Only Quentin knew about the flash drive and that Gina's attack wasn't some random incident. He clearly hadn't mentioned it to Val. He had to have a reason to keep it from her, so Gina stayed mum.

"I was hoping you could tell me if Quentin was home the night I was attacked," she said, moving on.

Val's brow furrowed. "You know he was here. He came over when he heard the gunshot."

"I mean before that."

"No, he went out with the guys and got home just after the shot was fired. He came in long enough to tell me to stay put while he checked on you, and then was out the door again." Val tilted her head, her gaze not leaving Gina's face.

"Where'd he'd go with his friends?"

"I don't know." Val pursed her lips and studied Gina. "Why all the questions about Quentin?"

Feeling guilty of suspecting her friend's husband, Gina waved her hand to dismiss Val's concern. "Nothing really. I was just wondering if he saw anything."

Val didn't buy it for a minute. "He's already told you he didn't."

"I know, but on those cop shows they always say people remember things later."

Val's concern faded. "I'd ask him for you, but by the time he gets home, I'll be sound asleep."

"I've been thinking about his boat." Gina's transition was so obvious, she held her breath waiting for Val to become suspicious again.

"What, the other woman in his life?" Val smiled.

Gina chuckled, appreciative as always of Val's good humor. She just couldn't imagine that a man married to her good friend would have killed Jon and attacked her. What could drive him to do such a thing?

*Money.* Derrick's word came barreling into her head.

Despite her affection for Val and Quentin, she had to keep digging. "You never said how he was able to afford such an expensive boat."

"No, we didn't." Val bit her lip.

Gina could see she had pushed too hard, but she couldn't give up now. "Mind if I ask you about it?"

Val appraised Gina for a moment. "What does his boat have to do with anything?"

Gina searched for a quick answer that wouldn't make Val suspicious.

Val held up her hand. "You know what? It doesn't matter. If you want to know anything about the boat, you'll have to take it up with Quentin."

"What? When?" Derrick shouted into his phone.

Gina spun in time to see him shove his fingers in his hair and start pacing.

"Looks like bad news," Val said.

More bad news? Gina was nearing the end of her rope. Barely keeping it together. How could she possibly handle more?

Derrick jammed his phone into his pocket and took purposeful strides in their direction. Gina swallowed hard and waited for him to join them.

"We need to go," he said, his eyes filled with worry that stole Gina's breath. Until this point, he'd never displayed even an ounce of fear.

Her stomach ached as she asked, "What's wrong?"

He laid a hand on her shoulder, but even his touch couldn't calm her worry.

"Kat needs us back at the hotel," he said. "Someone broke into the suite and tried to abduct Sophia."

# NINE

Derrick's heart slammed against his chest as he and Gina rushed to his car. He'd managed an outwardly calm appearance to keep Gina from falling apart, but he'd barely kept it together inside.

These unexpected attacks were starting to get to him. He needed a schedule with alarms and reminders to keep things in control. Not this insane free-for-all. He'd thought the multiple attacks on Gina were hard to handle, but this time they'd almost lost Sophia. *Little Bug.* If not for the baby monitor alerting Kat…

*No.* He wouldn't go there.

The monitor *had* alerted Kat, and Sophia was safe. Still, he needed to see her smiling face with his own two eyes before his worry would fade. Gina had the same—greater—need, but he wouldn't take her to Sophia unless he could do so safely, and that meant added precautions.

He opened the back door of the car. "Later, I'll need you to lie down on the floor, so be prepared."

She looked at him. "I didn't have to do that on the way here."

"The attempt to take Sophia changed everything." He helped her into the car and slammed the door before she questioned him again and delayed their departure.

"What aren't you telling me?" she asked the moment he slid behind the wheel.

As he cranked the engine, he glanced in his mirror. There was no point lying to her, not when the situation was so dangerous. "We're worried that this wasn't actually an attempt to abduct Sophia. We think your attacker might have staged the event so you'd come running."

Her eyes widened. "And when I arrive, he'll try to kill me again."

"Exactly." Derrick backed out of the space. "I don't really want to take you to the hotel, but I know you need to see Sophia."

"I wish I didn't, but I won't relax until I have her in my arms," she said, looking pensive. "Could Kat bring her to us?"

He shook his head. "The police are on scene, and she can't leave until they finish processing it. Since it's an attempted child abduction, that could take hours."

"Do you think it's safe for me to go there?"

"As safe as it can be under the circumstances," he said. "Kat arranged for us to park in the underground service entrance. But we have to get to the entrance first."

"And if this creep really is a trained sniper, he could fire a lethal shot," Gina finished for him, her voice surprisingly calm.

"So when we get closer to the hotel and I tell you to lie down, I need you to do so." He exited the apartment building's parking lot and merged into traffic.

"You won't have to tell me twice," she said with vehemence.

He was pleased with how well she was taking the attempted abduction, but he didn't want her to think about it all the way to the hotel. He glanced in the mirror. "Did you learn anything in your conversation with Valerie?"

"A few things actually." She leaned over the passenger seat. "Quentin went out the night I was attacked and came home just after the attack. Val said he was out with the guys, so at this point he doesn't have a solid alibi."

"That keeps him at the top of my suspect list until we can confirm his whereabouts." Derrick honestly hadn't wanted to believe Gina's friend was involved, but he felt good about having a suspect to investigate. "Did you ask about the money for his boat?"

"Yes, but I did a horrible job questioning her. She said I'd have to ask Quentin about it." Gina rested her chin on her arm.

Derrick moved into the turn lane. "I'd hoped she might be more open without me standing there."

"So that's why you left us alone."

He nodded. "Plus when she mentioned Quentin was out of town, I knew he could've flown to Portland and attacked you. So I wanted Ethan to start checking flight records."

"Val really seemed like she thought he was deployed."

"Which is why I also asked Cole to see if his military sources could confirm that. If they can, it will give Quentin an alibi for the Portland attack."

Gina shook her head. "I'm continually amazed at how fast you all think of these things."

"That's what we do and do well," he said, not surprised when he heard the pride for his family's skills and successes lodged in his voice.

"It sounds like you really love your job."

"Yeah. I mean, there are times when I'd rather not work with my brothers and sisters. You've spent enough time with us, so I'm sure I don't have to tell you why." He winked at her in the mirror.

"After the way I grew up, it's refreshing to see a committed family." A long sigh slipped from her mouth. "I hate that Sophia won't have a brother or sister."

He braked at a red light and looked back at her. "What happened to your plan of having a houseful of children?"

She shrugged.

Surprised, he angled himself so he could look into her eyes. "Something change?"

"Age and experience, I guess. Finding that perfect someone to have a family with isn't as easy as I thought it'd be." She firmly met his gaze. "You obviously know that since you're still single. Or don't you want to get married?"

How could he answer? Years ago, she'd accused him of always pulling away when things started to get serious, and she'd been right. Even after all this time, he hadn't resolved his problem. And that meant that despite his dreams of family, he'd always be on his own.

Anxious to see and hold Sophia, Gina rushed into the hotel room without so much as a glance at the police officers and forensic team. Kat held the smiling child as she talked with the same detective who'd responded to Gina's attack the other night. When Kat spotted Gina, she started across the room, and Gina met her halfway. She didn't need to ask for Sophia. Kat immediately handed her over.

"I'm sorry," Kat said, first looking at Gina then Derrick, who'd come up behind her. "The creep tried to come in through the bedroom window. I should've stationed myself in Sophia's room. But thankfully, I heard a noise on the baby monitor and went to check before he opened the window all the way."

"Did you get a good look at him?" Derrick asked.

Kat shook her head. "Caught a quick glimpse of his head and upper torso only. He wore a mask. Couldn't even get a good sense of his size except that he has broad shoulders. By the time I got to the window, he'd darted behind shrubs. I couldn't leave Sophia alone to chase him, so he got away."

"I hope you're not blaming yourself for this." Gina searched Sophia for any injuries. "You had no way of knowing this monster had found us."

"Hey, Bug," Derrick crooned over Gina's shoulder. "Sorry for the scare, but you're fine, aren't you?"

Sophia gave him a big, toothy grin and held her arms out to him. Gina wasn't ready to give her up, but her powerful little legs thrashed about, so she passed her to Derrick. She expected him to joke with Sophia or jiggle her, but what she didn't expect was for him to cradle her gently against his shoulder while sighing out a long breath. Sophia snuggled closer and contentedly plopped her thumb in her mouth.

"I'm so glad you're okay," he whispered. Then, as if he suddenly realized people were watching him, his expression morphed into his usual tough-guy facade and he started firing questions at Kat about the incident.

Gina tried to pay attention, but the only thing that was important to her right now was that the man didn't make it through the window and he didn't touch Sophia. Once she was sure of those facts, she focused on Sophia and Derrick again and questions flew through her mind. Would Derrick be a good father? One who would attend ballet and piano recitals, get up in the night with a sick child and walk the floor with her? Teach her how to drive and interview her first boyfriend?

A vision of Derrick, his hand clamped on his gun and this hard look trained on a potential boyfriend, made Gina smile.

Sophia had taken to him and he to her. Babies had good instincts. Gina honestly believed he'd be an excellent father. The opposite of her father.

*But you know better.*

He might love a child. Might be a caring and tender man, but he wouldn't provide the stability a child needed any more than her father had.

"Did you hear me, Gina?" Kat asked.

Gina snapped her focus to Kat. "No, sorry. I was too busy thinking about Sophia."

"Most rental cars today have GPS trackers installed for security reasons," Kat said. "We're thinking the attacker found us by tracking the car. We'll have Dani see if he could somehow access this data and check for a security breach in their system."

Gina thought about it. "If that's true, why didn't he follow us to the apartment?"

"Only he could know that," Derrick said. "But I suspect the thought of setting this trap and lying in wait for you here was the better option."

"Then thank you for thinking ahead," Gina said earnestly.

Derrick didn't acknowledge her thanks but said, "Ethan's arranging for a clean car and for us to stay with his friend Tracy Walden from the FBI. She'll pick you and Sophia up as soon as she can get free."

"You'll go with us, right?" The plea flew from Gina's lips, sounding needy and distraught—things Gina hated being.

"Yes. Kat will deliver our rental car to another hotel. She made a reservation there using my credit card. Hopefully your attacker will think we're holed up inside and watch the wrong location."

Moving Sophia again would be a hassle, but Gina would find a way to deal. "What about our things? Can we take them with us, or will the police need to look at everything first?"

Kat and Derrick shared an uneasy look.

"What's wrong now?" Gina asked.

Kat took a step closer and lowered her voice. "Detective Paulson doesn't seem very motivated to investigate. He thinks this may be another hoax."

Gina looked at the detective as he lounged on the other side of the room, barely bothering to process the scene. How could such a detective keep his job?

Anger mounting, she faced Kat. "I get that he doesn't believe me, but you're a former cop. I thought he'd at least believe you."

"It's not all that surprising," Kat replied. "Cops aren't always fond of investigators. They feel like we get in the way. Even more so with a former cop turned P.I. They take our career change personally. Like we've sold out."

Gina crossed her arms and looked back at the

detective. She didn't know what she'd have to do to convince him to take this seriously, but she'd certainly try her best. They needed all the help they could get to find this creep before he succeeded in harming her or Sophia.

Derrick hated not having Gina next to him. Not that she was far away. Just down the hall in one of Tracy's bedrooms with Sophia. Though Sophia had long ago fallen asleep, Gina refused to leave her alone. He didn't blame her. He'd reacted so powerfully when he'd held Sophia in his arms, he'd insisted that Gina leave the door open so he could make sure they were both safe.

"They'll be okay, you know." Kat packed the forensic samples they'd collected at the hotel and at Gina's apartment into an overnight shipping box for the lab.

"How do you know what I was thinking?"

"Please. You're the easiest one in the family to read." She thumped him on the head. "You've always been an open book and always will be."

Derrick stared up at her. "If I give everything away, then explain how I was such a successful detective."

She sealed the box. "I didn't say you were an open book at work. Just when your emotions are involved."

"This *is* work," he said, trying to convince himself. "We're charged with making sure nothing happens to them, and I'm concerned for their safety."

Kat met his gaze and held it. "It's more than concern. You're letting Gina get to you again. And don't get me started on what that precious baby is doing to you. You're gaga over the little sweetie."

He thought to deny both of her comments, but he'd be lying and he wouldn't disrespect his sister that way. But he also wouldn't discuss Gina when his feelings for her were a jumbled mess in his mind.

"Maybe you should go sit with them," he said. "That way you can quit distracting me, and I can get some research done on Perry Axton's death."

"Ha! Like *I'm* the distraction."

He glared at her. "Just go. I'm sure Gina would like the company."

"Fine, but let me know if you find anything out about Perry so I can prepare before tomorrow's interview." She put the box on the table and gave it a pat before leaving the room.

Derrick turned his back to the bedroom and forced his mind on to the story he'd been reading on his computer. Kat had scheduled an appointment to talk to the San Diego police detective in charge of Perry's case, but Derrick believed in learning all he could as soon as he could, so he'd started his own research, beginning with the long list of news stories about Perry's death. Derrick scanned the list and chose several posts to read. Learning nothing new, he skimmed through a few more stories, and on the last one, his mouth fell open. He reread the text.

"Crazy," he whispered. Their investigation had just taken an interesting turn, and he wasn't sure what to make of it, other than Gina was in even more peril than he could've imagined possible.

"I completed my rounds and everything's quiet," Tracy said, coming into the room. Still dressed in her work clothes—a nondescript gray pantsuit with a white blouse—the agent stopped next to Derrick. "Research?"

He nodded. "You know anything about Renato Ontiveros?"

"Sure, everyone in law enforcement around here knows about Ontiveros. He's a particularly ruthless drug runner." She pulled out a chair and sat. "Why the interest in him?"

"He was initially arrested for the murder of Perry Axton when the CG team tried to board his boat."

She rested her elbows on the table. "With his illegal activities, it'd make sense that he returned fire when they tried to apprehend him."

"You know anything else about him?"

"He's been suspected in a number of heinous murders, but he's skated every time." Her eyes creased. "If he's the man after Gina, then the stakes in this case have just escalated exponentially."

Derrick glanced at the screen again and looked at Ontiveros's mug shot. "I don't have proof that he's our man."

"What say I make a pot of coffee and you, Kat and I sit down to talk about it?"

"That'd be good." Derrick glanced toward Gina's bedroom. "But let's keep this conversation between the three of us for now. No sense in worrying Gina unless we're certain a ruthless killer like Ontiveros is indeed the man trying to end her life."

# TEN

Derrick pulled into the parking garage at Gina's apartment building the next day and peered in the rearview mirror to confirm Gina remained out of sight. She hadn't wanted to leave Sophia with Kat, but when Tracy volunteered to stay, Gina capitulated.

After the information Derrick had discovered on Ontiveros, he would've gladly left Gina at Tracy's house with its higher security. But without Gina, he wouldn't get anywhere in questioning Quentin. And Derrick wasn't about to bring their number one suspect to the safe house for questioning.

"You can sit up now." Derrick parked in the apartment garage and turned to Gina. "Not that I have to tell you this, but stay close by my side. We'll go straight inside."

She nodded, but she was clearly distracted.

"I get that you're worried about Sophia, but two capable professionals are protecting her." He waited for Gina to look at him or say something, but she didn't respond. He placed his hand over hers resting on the seatback and waited until she met his gaze. "I need you here, Gina. Now. In the present. Not distracted. If your attacker has somehow followed us, you need to be able to react at a moment's notice. Can you do that for me?"

She nodded, but it was a weak gesture.

"Do you want to call Kat and confirm Sophia's fine before we go inside?"

Her eyes brightened. "Can I?"

"Of course." He dialed Kat and handed over his phone.

"What's wrong, Derrick?" Kat's voice was so loud Derrick heard it in the front.

"It's Gina and nothing's wrong. I just wanted to make sure everything was okay with Sophia."

He couldn't hear Kat's response, but the glimmer of a smile on Gina's lips said the house was secure. His heart did a silly little flip-flop from the smile she'd rarely displayed the past few days.

"Thank you for being so understanding, Kat," Gina said. "I promise not to call you again for at least five minutes." She said goodbye and handed the phone back to him. "Thank you, too. I know I'm overreacting, but she's just a helpless baby."

He stowed his phone. "Believe me, I don't want anything to happen to Bug either."

"You're going to be a wonderful father." The sincerity in her voice caught him by surprise.

"Not anytime soon," he said quickly before he

allowed her suggestion to give him hope for something he'd never have. "Ready to do this?"

"Yes." Confusion lingered on her face, likely from the way he'd shut her down, but he wasn't going to discuss it.

Outside, he secured his arm around her. Though it was for safety, he was growing fond of having her by his side. He kept her snugly in his care until Quentin answered the door and greeted them cordially.

Derrick didn't buy the pleasant act. Around six-two and built like a linebacker, Quentin fit the description of Gina's attacker, and Derrick wouldn't take his eyes off the man. Not for a second or even a nanosecond. Bad things happened that fast and left people scarred for life.

Quentin stepped back and Gina headed inside. Derrick followed but stationed himself in the entryway. From this location, he could see Gina continue into the toy-cluttered family room yet still view Quentin as he closed the door.

"You can have a seat, man," Quentin said as he passed Derrick.

Derrick leaned against the wall to convey a sense of ease but remained on high alert. "No, thanks, I'm good."

"Suit yourself." Quentin plopped onto a leather chair made for his large size.

Gina sat on a sofa in the middle of the room. "Where are Val and the kids?"

"Val said you wanted to talk about the night you

were attacked, so I thought it'd be better if we didn't have little ears listening in." Quentin leaned forward and propped his elbows on his knees. "Is that why you're here? To talk about that night?"

"Partially," Gina said. "There've been additional incidents since that night." As she recounted Lilly's murder, her voice trembled and her eyes filled with pain.

Derrick couldn't stand to see her distress and do nothing about it, so he crossed the room and stood behind her. Hopefully she felt his support, even if he didn't reach out and touch her.

"I'm sorry about all of this, Gina," Quentin said. "I didn't know your friend, though, so I'm not sure how I can help." Derrick hated to admit it, but the guy sounded sincere.

"It's not just Lilly." Gina's voice was growing stronger. "The same man shot at me in Portland and almost killed me, too. Then he tried to abduct Sophia yesterday."

Quentin winced and ran a hand around the back of his neck. "Whoever's doing this seems pretty determined to get to you. Maybe you should find someplace safe where he'll never locate you." He looked at Derrick. "If you care about Gina and Sophia, you'll get them out of San Diego today."

"So you think the danger is focused here? Sounds like there's something you know about this but aren't telling us," Derrick said, keeping his cool when he wanted to shake the man to get him to quit talking in circles. "Like maybe you have more information about the attack in Gina's apartment."

"As I told Gina that night, I don't know anything that can help. But it doesn't take a rocket scientist to see this guy means business. She'd be better off away from it all."

Gina peered at Quentin. "The attacker broke in to get Jon's flash drive. If we can figure out what the log Jon put on the drive means, we might be able to catch this man once and for all." Gina coupled her plea with an imploring look. "Please help us, Quentin. You have to know something. Otherwise, why did you ask to look through Jon's belongings? You must know what the log is for."

"I'm sorry." He looked away. "There's nothing I can do."

He was lying. His body language cinched it in Derrick's mind. But if Gina's plea didn't get the man to speak, Derrick couldn't change Quentin's mind and it was time to move on. "Perhaps you can tell us about Perry Axton's death?"

Quentin whipped around to look at Derrick. "What's Perry's death got to do with this?"

"We're not sure yet," Derrick said, playing it cool. "What can you tell us about how he died?"

"Not a whole lot to tell. He was killed on a drug raid. All of us saw him go down. It was dark, and no one caught a clear view of the shooter. We hoped to convict the gang leader we arrested for it, but that didn't pan out."

"You're talking about Renato Ontiveros." Derrick was glad he'd decided to forewarn Gina about Ontiveros.

Quentin nodded. "If you know his name, then you know he's bad news. The team would've liked to see him go away for life, but when the bullet that killed Perry didn't match Ontiveros's weapon, there was nothing anyone could do, including the police." Quentin sat forward. "That's really all I can tell you. I'd like to join the kids at that park. So if you're finished…"

*Not so fast.* "Your wife told us you went out of town after the attack on Gina."

"Yeah, so?"

"Where'd you go?"

Quentin crossed his arms. "That's classified."

Derrick could tell the guy was digging in his heels. It was time to cut to the chase. "Is the source of the money for your boat classified, too?"

Quentin cast a pained look at Gina then came to his feet and planted his boots wide. "If you suspect me of something, come right out and say it. If not, we're done."

"Did you have anything to do with Jon's death?" Derrick asked, surprising the man.

"No." He gestured at the door. "It's time for you to go."

"Please, Quentin." Gina stood. "Can you at least tell me where you went the night I was attacked so we can prove you aren't involved?"

He firmed his jaw and shook his head before heading to the door and jerking it open. They stepped outside.

"Get her out of town, man." After a last look at Gina, Quentin closed the door.

"That didn't go so well," Gina said.

"I don't know," Derrick replied. "At least we learned he was on Perry's last raid. He could've killed him with friendly fire. And we know he's hiding something."

"So I didn't imagine it then. He really *is* acting weird."

Derrick settled her under his arm again and started down the hall. "I don't know how he usually behaves, but if I'd hauled him in for interrogation when I was on the force, I wouldn't have let him leave until he'd told me what he was hiding."

She looked up at him, searching his face. "Too bad you're not a detective, or you could detain him."

"Trust me," Derrick said with all the confidence he could muster. "I'll still figure out what he's hiding. It'll just be more of a challenge."

Gina knew Dani was arriving today, but she was still surprised to see her in Tracy's kitchen with Kat when they returned. Sophia lay on her back on Dani's long legs as Dani bent down and planted kisses on Sophia's face. She giggled and Gina felt the first genuine smile surface since the near abduction, making her content to stand and watch them.

Derrick didn't seem to have as much patience but marched past Gina and knuckled Dani on the head. "Glad you got here okay."

She looked up. "Oh, hi. I didn't hear you two over the giggles." Dani changed her focus to Gina. "I hope you don't mind. I caught an earlier flight so I took over for Tracy. Of course, that included smooching this little one's cheeks."

"I don't mind at all," Gina replied sincerely. "I'm glad to see her having fun."

"I promised Ethan we'd do a video conference as soon as you got back." Dani lifted Sophia to her feet and handed her to Gina then opened her computer.

Gina's good mood evaporated. "That doesn't sound good."

"He just wants to update us." Kat was already logging on to her computer.

Derrick pulled out a chair for Gina, and she sat while Sophia grasped Gina's thumbs and balanced on her toes. As Dani's computer whirred through the conferencing program, Gina's stomach knotted. She'd come to expect the worst since her attack, and she didn't like the feeling at all.

*Father, please help me to remain positive and strong.*

Derrick dragged a chair next to her. Sophia reached for him. Gina didn't even bother to fight it this time and let her climb into Derrick's arms. He tossed her in the air and had her giggling again.

Ethan's face appeared on the screen. "I thought you all were working there, not playing house."

"You know what they say," Kat responded. "All work and no play—"

"I wish you'd come home to play," Mitch's voice sounded over the computer speaker.

"Mitch?" Kat's voice lifted in excitement. "If you're there, show that handsome face on the screen."

"Yes, Mitch," Derrick joked as he peeked around Sophia. "Show us that so-called handsome face."

Scowling, Mitch appeared on the screen. "You'll pay for that comment when you get home, pretty boy."

"Pretty boy?" Gina asked and got a similar scowl from Derrick.

"Mitch thinks Derrick is too pretty." Dani's eyes lit with humor.

Gina pretended to seriously study him. "They're right. You do look a lot like Dani, and she's very pretty."

"Not you, too." Derrick groaned and Gina laughed. "Thanks a lot, Mitch."

"That's what brothers-in-law are for." Mitch smiled, transforming the mock-sour expression he'd worn earlier.

"Hi," Kat said dreamily and touched Mitch's face on the screen.

"Hey," Mitch answered in a similar tone. The jealousy that bit into Gina when watching Luke and Dani reared its ugly head again.

"Do you two need us to leave the room for a minute?" Dani asked fondly.

Kat turned to her sister. "I guarantee if Luke's face was on the screen you wouldn't be such a smart aleck."

Dani winked. "Maybe you could invite him to join our next call, and I'll let you know."

A rapid-fire exchange occurred with each sibling one-upping the other with quick-witted statements. Gina forgot all of her troubles for a moment and smiled along with them. Even Sophia joined in, laughing when the others cracked up.

How wonderful being a part of a family like this would be. It was something Gina had longed for all her life. Something she wanted for Sophia. Something Gina was determined to give her. But how was that possible without making herself vulnerable again? Without trusting someone?

Cole stuck his face in front of the camera, and his smile disappeared. "Anyone mind if we get some work done so the rest of us can get home to our significant others?"

"Good thinking," Ethan said. "I'll start. I've reviewed Jon's and Quentin's credit card statements and discovered they've been in a host of ports in the past six months. I'll email the list to Dani to match to the data you recover from Jon's hard drive. Maybe we'll get lucky and figure out where he received the log."

"I've been a bit distracted by this little one since

I got here." Dani turned and tickled Sophia. "But I promise to work on the drive as soon as we hang up."

"So what you're telling us," Ethan said, "is that we'll get no work out of you once you have a child of your own."

She grinned. "Sounds about right."

Ethan shook his head. "That's it for me. Who's up next?"

Kat raised her hand. "I struck out on finding any injury reports that match our guy. Either Gina's attacker wasn't hit or he didn't seek medical care. Also, I've put a rush on the blood sample we sent to the lab, and hopefully we'll get the results back soon."

"I'll be glad to run the DNA through our databases to search for a match," Mitch offered. "Did you get the reports I faxed for Jon's crash?"

Kat nodded. "They're pretty straightforward and list no indication of foul play. I've scheduled a meeting with the detective in charge of the case, and I'll take a look at the car if it's still impounded. Maybe I'll see something they missed."

"What about the car that followed us from the airport, Mitch?" Derrick asked while Sophia played with her feet. "You get any info on their crash?"

"The men fled before the police arrived, and the car's a rental. We tracked it to the agency, but it was rented with bogus credentials. The detectives are still trying to locate the men, but so far it's a dead end."

"Speaking of rental cars." Dani looked at Derrick.

"Yours was equipped with a tracker, but I wasn't able to determine if the agency's records were hacked."

"You, unable to figure something out?" Cole asked.

She wrinkled her nose. "I could go into detail on the reason, as I know how all of you love my details."

A collective groan came from the siblings.

"Suffice it to say it's another dead end."

"Par for the course," Derrick said, and Gina didn't like to hear how dejected he sounded.

"I appreciate the work all of you have done," she interjected, hoping to bring back Derrick's optimism. "Even if you've hit dead ends."

"Not all of us have struck out." Cole leaned forward. "I've learned a few things about Quentin. He's very well trained in a variety of weaponry. As Gina said, he's the team's best marksman. He also holds sharpshooting awards. He definitely needs to remain on the top of our suspect list."

"I agree." Derrick set Sophia on his lap, and she started bouncing. "Gina and I just questioned him. He admitted to being on the raid where Perry was killed. He claims his location since the attack is classified, and he won't say anything about the money for his boat."

"Plus his wife told me he'd gone out on the night of my attack, returning home just after the gunshot was fired, but he won't tell us where he was," Gina said.

"And he was MIA during the Portland shooting," Derrick added.

Ethan frowned. "So far I haven't found him on any commercial-flight manifests."

"I'm still working on verifying his deployment," Cole said. "That's gonna take some time, and I'm not sure I have the right contacts to get that information, but I'll keep after it."

"Gina, are you any more convinced that he might be guilty?" Ethan asked.

"I don't want to believe it, but he's behaving so oddly that I have to suspect him."

"Then he remains our best lead," Ethan said. "Does anyone have anything else? If not, I called this meeting so Mitch could share information with all of us at the same time."

"Go ahead, honey," Kat purred.

"Yes, honey," Cole mocked. "Please do."

Rolling his eyes, Mitch came on the screen. "I'm afraid I have bad news to report."

Gina's heart sank. "It's about Lilly, isn't it?

"I'm sorry, Gina," he said. "We recovered her body downriver."

Pained by the confirmation, Gina couldn't get out a word.

Dani took Gina's hand. "We're all sorry for your loss."

Gina nodded, but she still couldn't speak. She groped for her purse and dug a tissue out while she composed herself. "Was I right? Did he shoot her?"

Mitch nodded gravely. "Her autopsy is scheduled for tomorrow. We'll recover the slug at that time and compare it with the ballistic test for the one we removed from Derrick's houseboat."

Gina sighed. Lilly had actually died. Was murdered.

*Unreal.*

Breath-stealing panic climbed up Gina's throat. These brave men and women may use terms such as *autopsy* and *ballistics tests* every day, but Gina didn't. Now they were words that hit close to home. Too close. And after hearing about so many dead ends in the investigation, she worried the killer would strike again before they discovered his identity. This time, she feared he'd strike even closer.

# ELEVEN

Derrick stood in the family room doorway and watched Gina. His anger flared at the senseless loss of life—and at the way it had upset Gina so much she'd fled the conference call. He'd started to follow her, but his number one job was to find the murderer. Working toward that meant sitting through the rest of the call.

Still, even as he'd settled Sophia in her crib for a nap, his mind centered on Gina's loss. He got how she felt. He'd mourned friends, too. Everyone in the family had, in various ways. Plus all of them shared the loss of their adoptive parents when they were murdered.

He curled his hands into fists. He'd wanted to rail at the injustice then, and he wanted to do so now. But his anger didn't help. Never helped.

Nothing had. Not even time, really. He still missed his birth parents after twenty-one years despite comfort from Dani—and from his adoptive family.

He hated that Gina had to go through this again.

Especially so soon after losing her sister-in-law and her brother. He couldn't just stand here. He had to help even if it meant crossing the line of professionalism.

Forcing his hands to relax, he approached the sofa. She looked up, the agony on her face searing his heart. He wanted to draw her into his arms. To hold and comfort her. With their past, he should back away, but how could he not show her he understood? That he'd do just about anything to take this pain from her?

He sat on the sofa next to her. "I'm so sorry about Lilly."

Gina dabbed a tissue under her eyes. "It's what I expected, but actually hearing it confirmed is another story."

He took her hand. "Is there anything I can do?"

She shook her head, and as her crying ramped up again, she moved to the fireplace, her back to him.

*Enough. No matter your past or fear of getting involved again, she needs you.*

He went to her and turned her by the shoulders. She looked him square in the face, her tearstained eyes meeting his. Slowly, so she could move away if she chose, he slid his hands down her arms and around her waist. She didn't back away but readily moved nearer. He drew her close, and she rested her head on his chest.

As her crying intensified, he stroked her hair and whispered comforting words he hoped would help.

As much as he wanted to offer comfort right now, he selfishly thought about the last time he'd held her while she'd truly relied on him. College, so long ago. A time before her ultimatum that she would leave if he didn't commit.

What would his life be like today if he'd worked through his commitment issues? Would he have someone like Gina and a child like Sophia in his life? He wanted to change now more than ever, but he'd tried for years to no avail. He couldn't do this on his own.

*Father, give me clarity on this issue. Show me what to do so I don't spend the rest of my life alone.*

The alarm on Derrick's phone split the quiet, opening Gina's eyes. She pushed away from the sculptured wall of his chest and instantly felt alone and vulnerable again. Had she come to depend on him in such a short time? Did this mean she couldn't cope alone anymore? Didn't want to cope?

*Please don't let that be true.*

Derrick trailed a hand down her arm. "I'm sorry to leave you right now, but I need to take off if I'm to meet the detective on time."

"I thought Kat was going."

"She was. Before I discovered the information on Ontiveros." His eyes narrowed. "I need to hear firsthand what the detective has to say."

"I'd like to go, too," she said. "Jon never gave me

classified details, but he talked about work. I might catch something the detective says that you miss."

Derrick shook his head. "The police aren't taking your complaints seriously, and if you're with me, they won't take me seriously either."

"But they already know you're working with me."

"Hopefully without you physically present, they'll focus on the details of the case."

She sighed, and her shoulders slumped slightly. "I don't agree with you, but if that's what you think is best, I'll accept your decision and stay here."

"Thank you." He twined his fingers with hers.

"Promise you'll call me if you need clarification on anything the detective says."

"I promise." He squeezed her hand and, after a sweet smile, he departed.

Gina turned to find Kat watching her.

"It's time we had a chat." Kat tipped her head at the kitchen. "Let's have a cup of coffee while we talk."

Having no idea what Kat wanted to say, Gina followed her to the kitchen. Gina sat while Kat retrieved two steaming mugs of coffee.

She took a seat across the table then stirred sugar into her cup. "I won't stand by and watch while you hurt Derrick again."

"What?" Gina fell back on her chair. "Where's that coming from?"

Kat set down her spoon and looked up. "The two of you have changed in the past few days. Especially

Derrick. He was wary of you at first. Now he's put that behind him."

"That's a good thing."

"Good?" Kat shrugged. "Maybe or maybe not."

"I don't follow."

"You know him. He's the first to stand up and defend anyone who's been wronged. But I suspect he's confusing that protectiveness with affection for you, and I'm afraid you're leading him on only to bail on him again."

Gina tried not to take offense at Kat's blunt statement. In fact, she respected her for speaking her mind, but that didn't mean she was right. "I have no intention of leading him on. I simply want his help in resolving this matter so Sophia and I can live in peace."

"Great," Kat said. "Then we won't have any problems."

"You may not believe this, but I want to see Derrick happy." Gina grabbed her mug to keep her hands busy. "I don't intend to hurt him. He's a great guy and I loved him once, but I couldn't stay in a relationship that wasn't going anywhere."

"Which is even more reason to keep things professional now."

"Because he hasn't changed, you mean. He's still not ready to settle down." Gina sipped on her coffee as she waited for Kat to acknowledge his ongoing issue. She stared ahead and Gina took it as an unspoken confirmation.

Kat suddenly stood and stared down at Gina, a warning burning in her eyes. "Don't hurt him or you'll be dealing with me."

"Message received," Gina said.

Kat walked away and Gina let out a slow breath. She was glad Derrick's siblings were looking out for him—but who was on her side? Who'd defend her if Derrick's inability to commit hurt her again?

The answer was simple—no one. She'd just have to look out for herself. Which meant finding a way to ignore the feelings Derrick was bringing to the surface. Something she should readily want to do after her history with men.

So why was she hoping that Derrick was like her father and it wasn't too late for him to change?

*Stop it, Gina.* Thoughts like that only lead to self-destruction.

Thirty minutes into Derrick's conversation with Detective Gleason, Derrick wanted to wring the man's neck. He'd run Derrick in circles, not giving a straight answer to any question and refusing to share the case file for Perry Axton's murder. But Derrick wouldn't give up. Gina needed him to keep after Gleason, and that's what he'd do until the detective gave him answers or tossed him out.

He slid forward on his chair. "I'd hoped we'd be able to collaborate on this. You know, as one officer to another."

"Former officer," Gleason clarified and crossed

his arms over a burly chest. "You're not one of us now, are you?"

"Trust me," Derrick said sincerely, "I've been in your shoes, and I'd have refused to show my files to a guy like me, too. But it wouldn't violate any rules if you shared a little background information on the main suspect in the Axton case."

"Renato Ontiveros?"

"Yeah."

"You don't want to go anywhere near that guy." Gleason watched Derrick carefully. "You don't have a police force backing you up, and Ontiveros is one of the most ruthless men we've come across in a long time."

Derrick wanted to take Gleason's advice and leave Ontiveros alone, but that wasn't an option. "Has he ever been incarcerated?"

"Nah, he's lucked out. You know the type. Guilty as sin, but forensics always fail to prove it. Plus any potential witness against him is usually too afraid to talk."

Derrick thought about a killer like this coming after Gina, and a ball of dread formed in his gut. "I've worked a few cases like that. He lawyers up the minute you haul him in, right?"

Gleason snorted. "Ha, like we ever get to bring him in. He's so well hidden and protected we've never gotten to him. Only reason we got a crack at him for Axton's murder was thanks to the Coast Guard. They were doing a routine flyover and ended up raiding his boat."

"He didn't do time for the drugs recovered that day?"

"What drugs? They dumped everything before the Guard had a chance to board. No evidence, no conviction." Gleason stared at Derrick, his eyebrow suddenly quirking. "You didn't mention why you were looking into Axton in the first place."

"His teammate Jonathan Evans died in a car crash recently. He was looking into Axton's death and might have uncovered some crucial evidence. We think that someone ran him off the road to keep him quiet."

Gleason leaned his chair back and propped a foot on his desk. "What'd the investigation reveal?"

"Jon's crash was ruled an accident."

"If his case is related to Axton's—" Gleason held up his hand to ward off Derrick's interruption "—and without any knowledge of this Evans's case, I can't even speculate if it is, Ontiveros wouldn't think twice before killing your guy. In fact, we like Ontiveros for a case where his competitor was run off the road and died in a fiery crash."

*Great.* On the one hand, Derrick had hoped to locate information lending credence to their theory that Ontiveros could be Gina's attacker. On the other hand, Derrick had hoped a known killer wasn't their guy.

He needed to know if there was a connection to

Jon and Perry. "Are you willing to ask the detective who investigated Jon's crash about a connection to Axton and how Ontiveros might play into all of this?"

Gleason thought for a minute then let his shoe drop to the floor with a thud as he came to his feet. "Why not? No one wants Ontiveros incarcerated more than I do."

Knowing the interview was over, Derrick stood and clapped Gleason on the shoulder. "I appreciate your willingness to help."

Gleason frowned. "Now, don't go getting all sappy on me. I didn't say I'd reopen the investigation or get my fellow detective to do so. I just said I'd ask."

"I understand." Derrick pulled out his business card and laid it on the desk. "But it's a step in the right direction."

# TWELVE

Day three in the investigation dawned sunny. The warm rays filtering into Tracy's family room should have brightened Derrick's mood, but he wasn't any closer to finding the killer than he'd been the day Gina barged into his life. That left him frustrated. Beyond frustrated.

He glanced at Gina, sitting on the sofa. She wore a vibrant blue sweater and colorful scarf around her neck. An hour or so ago, she'd tucked her violin under her chin and played with such joy. The look on her face was serene. A feeling he longed for right now.

He should find a way to relax, too. At least take the edge off. But he couldn't. The fire to solve a case had never burned in his gut as fiercely as it did with this one. He wanted to solve it. Needed to solve it. For Gina and Sophia. For himself. For the ability to breathe freely again.

Gina shifted and the sun's rays caught her face. The urge to join her hit him hard. To share in her peaceful moment and just be with her, here and now. Or maybe longer. Maybe forever.

The revelation was a punch to the gut. Despite his attempts to remain detached, he'd let her into his heart again.

*So what're you gonna do about it?*

His phone chimed from the table, making Gina's bow fall from her violin. The silence between rings seemed deafening as he glanced at the caller ID, hoping Gleason was calling to offer information about Ontiveros. When Derrick spotted Ethan's picture, he released a breath.

"It's Ethan," he said, hoping it would help Gina relax again, but she settled her violin in the case, her gaze never leaving him.

Forcing a cheerful note in his voice, he answered his phone. "If you have good news to report, I'll put you on speaker so Gina can hear it."

"Then speaker it is," Ethan said.

Derrick joined Gina. "Go ahead, Ethan."

"I used registration records to track Quentin Metzger's boat purchase from a local dealership."

"I'll pay the dealer a visit then," Derrick said, hoping this lead would help prove Quentin was a more viable suspect than Ontiveros.

"I'll text you the company's name and address once we hang up."

"Excellent." Derrick smiled at Gina, and she returned it with a breathtaking smile of her own. The sun played on her hair, captivating him. He gladly forgot about his brother.

"Wish I had more to give you." Ethan's voice pulled him back. "I'll keep digging, but that's all I have for now."

"It's a great place to start. Thanks." Derrick clicked off to wait for the text.

"I'd like to go with you when you talk to the dealer."

"It's safer if you stay here."

She set her jaw. "We've been at Tracy's place a day now with no sign that my attacker has located us. So how would he know we were headed to a boat dealership?"

She was right. Derrick opened his mouth to say she could accompany him, but before he could utter a word, she took his hand.

"Please let me go. I can help. I've been on Quentin's boat, and I know him, which could get the dealer to open up with us." She clasped his hand tighter.

His phone chimed a text. "I'll agree on one condition."

"Name it."

He looked in her eyes to be sure she understood the importance of his request. "You lay down in the car again, and when we get to the dealership, I scope it out first. Any sign of a problem, and we hightail it out of there. Understood?"

"Understood." She smiled as she had a moment

ago, and his heart flipped over in a way only she could cause.

He glanced at the address and shoved his phone in his pocket. "Then let's get going."

After an uneventful drive, Derrick pulled into the busy marina and spotted the boat dealership at the far end of the pier. He parked as close to the entrance as possible and left the engine running.

Making a quick sweep of the area from his seat, he found nothing amiss. "Stay here and stay down until I finish my recon."

"Yes, sir," Gina said with a little giggle that made him smile.

Leaving the door ajar in case he needed to take off in a hurry, he lifted his binoculars and scanned the entire area then zoomed in on the dealership building. Shaped like a large houseboat with a crow's nest on the top, it jutted out into the bay on large pillars. A wraparound porch circled the structure, and boats of all sizes and shapes were moored at the long pier.

Very picturesque if they were here for pleasure, but that wasn't their goal. Too bad. He could see spending a day relaxing with Gina on a boat. The wind in her hair. A smile on her lips.

*Don't get distracted now of all times.*

He leaned in the car and killed the engine. "We're good to go. Stay—"

"Close to you and don't stop until we're inside," Gina finished for him as she sat up.

"Guess I've gotten a bit predictable." He closed his door and surveyed the area.

Gina moved confidently toward him and slipped under his arm as if the position was natural and right. Maybe she was coming to trust him again. Something that brought a smile to his face.

"What're you smiling about?" she asked as they set off.

"This peace and relief from the uneasiness between us."

"It feels better, doesn't it?"

He nodded then turned his focus back to keeping her safe. He guided her quickly across the lot and onto the porch, where a flock of seagulls chattered.

Gina turned in a circle, taking him with her. "This place is something else. I guess when you sell expensive boats, you have to have an expensive showroom."

"Is it hard to imagine Quentin shopping here?"

"Very." She peered at him. "I don't mean to disparage your work, but is there any way Ethan could be wrong?"

"No."

"Then we should get inside and start asking questions."

"Yes, ma'am," Derrick said in the same tone she'd used in the car.

She wrinkled her nose at him, and he had to fight the urge to kiss the cute little tip. Instead, he opened the door and stood back so she could enter.

The air-conditioned space displaying five large

boats was scented with coconut air freshener. A tall, silver-haired man with a deep tan and skin like leather jumped from behind a desk and marched up to them with his hand extended.

"Zeb Stevens. How can I help you?" He smiled earnestly.

Derrick returned the smile. "Our friend bought a boat here, and we wondered if we could talk to the person who sold it to him."

"Sure. We're always glad when a customer makes a referral."

Derrick didn't bother correcting Zeb's misconception.

"If you give me your friend's name, I can look it up."

"Quentin Metzger."

Zeb's smile widened. "Don't need to look up Quentin. I sold him the boat."

"You're sure?" Gina asked.

Zeb held up a hand. "I'm not trying to swoop in on someone else's commission. I really do know Quentin. Not often we get Coast Guarders in here, so I picked his brain about boats. Knowledgeable guy."

"Could you show us the model he bought?" Derrick asked, hoping to gather information subtly instead of risking making Zeb clam up.

"Of course. It's our most popular model." He gestured at the far end of the showroom. "Right over here."

"I'm going to pretend to be a buyer," Derrick whispered to Gina. "Play along, okay?"

"Do you know anything about boats?"

"Sure. They float."

She rolled her eyes. "I can't wait to see you pull this off."

Derrick didn't doubt his ability to act the part. Over the years, he'd successfully played many roles in his investigations, and he intended to succeed today, as well. He'd start by following his first rule—admit that he was a novice and praise the expert's skills. Most of them basked in feeling good about themselves and forgot all about the fact that he had no business asking the questions.

Zeb stopped near a sleek white boat with blue and yellow stripes racing down the side. "So tell me. What are you looking for in a boat?"

Derrick made solid eye contact. "Honestly, I don't know a thing about boats, but I love anything that goes fast."

"Don't we all." Zeb patted the boat as a father might pat his child's head. "Has Quentin taken you for a ride?"

Gina mocked a shiver. "I was surprised at how fast his boat travels."

Zeb stroked the side of the boat. "Don't let this baby's size fool you. She may be a thirty-four-footer, but she's designed for speed."

Derrick nodded to show his appreciation. "How much would a boat like this set me back?"

"She retails around ninety grand." Zeb took a step

closer and lowered his voice even though there wasn't another person in the room. "Your cost depends on how you want to pay for it. I can offer a 5 percent discount for cash up front."

Derrick turned to Gina. "Didn't Quentin say that's how he paid?"

Gina shrugged. "You know I don't listen when you guys talk about your toys."

*Impressive.* She was a good partner.

Zeb looked at Gina. "You're like a lot of the ladies who come in. You like riding in the boat, but you don't want to talk specifics." Zeb turned back to Derrick. "Quentin paid cash so I was able to give him a real sweet deal. Could do the same thing for you."

"That's a tempting offer, Zeb," Derrick said, letting his voice fall off in hopes that Gina would take up the charge.

She laid a hand on his arm. "You'd better not be thinking of dropping that kind of money without discussing it first."

Zeb smiled. "Maybe we should take her out on the water. Let you see how she performs."

Gina held up her hand. "Not today. I need to think about this first."

"You heard the lady." Derrick wrapped his arm around her shoulder and pulled her close to his side. "I wouldn't dream of doing anything she didn't first approve, so we'll have to get back to you."

Zeb dug out his business card and handed it to Derrick. "Call me if you decide to move forward. No one in town will beat my deal. No one."

Derrick kept his arm around Gina and escorted her out the door. Outside, he stopped and smiled at her. "You're very good at pretending."

She returned his smile, and his heart dipped for the second time that day. Their little charade reminded him of college, when they were a real couple and made decisions together. Until the day she left. That decision she made on her own.

He'd carried anger over that for years, but now he realized he didn't care a whit about it anymore. He simply wanted to spend time with her again. Get to know her again. See where this obvious connection between them would go. Would that be fair to her? Was he ready to make a commitment at last? He wasn't sure—but if he didn't try, he'd never find out.

He lifted his hand to her face. She frowned and opened her mouth to speak, but before any words could come out—

The retort of a gun split the quiet, and a bullet whizzed between them.

Derrick reacted quickly, tackling Gina to the ground. Another bullet zipped overhead into the railing, the shot coming from a boat on the water. A sudden roar of a high-speed motor followed, bringing the craft closer to shore.

Derrick covered Gina's body and made a quick

assessment. The boat was closing in fast—he had to move her out of harm's way.

The motor suddenly wound down. Had the shooter retreated?

Another retort sounded through the air, and the bullet missed Derrick's arm by inches. The shooter hadn't retreated at all. He'd stopped to take better aim. The boat's motor roared to life again, bringing the shooter closer still. They hadn't a moment to lose.

Derrick had to get them out of this situation right away. But where could they go?

They couldn't get up and run to the shore, nor could they return to the showroom. Both options would leave them too exposed. His heart thudded in his chest as his mind sought a solution that minimized the danger to Gina.

*Come on, Justice. Think.*

He searched the area again, and a crazy idea popped into his head. A high-risk idea, exposing him to a bullet in the back, but it was better than remaining here and waiting for a sure death. He might not make it, but Gina would have a good chance. He had to risk it.

If he didn't, when the shooter got close enough for a kill shot, they'd both be dead.

# THIRTEEN

Gina tried not to panic, but when another bullet pierced the railing inches from her head, her heart thundered in her chest. She felt Derrick's beat a similar rhythm.

"We're not safe here," he said. "We have to move."

"Back inside?" she asked.

"No. We'll never make it. Our only hope is to jump off the pier."

"What?" She turned and sought his eyes. "Into the water? But won't that make us even more vulnerable?"

"Bullets lose velocity the minute they hit water and can veer off course. Our chances are better in the water than up here."

"Couldn't it do the opposite and redirect a bullet at us?"

"It's possible, but it's a better option than lying here and waiting for him to move close enough for a guaranteed shot."

She didn't know why she was questioning him. He

was the expert and he'd kept her safe so far. "If that's your assessment then I trust you."

He squeezed her hand. "The railing opening is too narrow for both of us to fit through at the same time. You go first and I'll cover you."

"But that'll leave you exposed."

"Don't worry about that. Just keep your head down and when you get to the edge, jump. After you surface, find the nearest pylon and move under the pier."

The thought of him taking a bullet for her left her breathless. "I can't let you do this. It's too dangerous to you."

"I know the risk, and I know it will work." He cupped the side of her face. "Trust me. Okay?"

She did trust him, but could she stand to lose him now that they'd reconnected?

*Lord, keep him safe,* she pleaded.

He removed his hand and her confidence fled. She clutched his arm. "You're sure about this?"

"Positive."

"Okay then."

"We need to shed our jackets or they'll weigh us down," he instructed. "Your vest will take on a little water, but keep it on." He helped her ease out of her coat then he removed his.

"He has the motor wide open, which means he's on the move and can't get off a good shot. So at the count of three, I'll roll off and we go. Ready?"

She nodded, and before she could say or do anything, he lowered his head and kissed her. A quick, to-the-point, no-nonsense kiss, but it helped her relax.

"For good luck." He lifted his head and grinned. "One."

He rose up on his arms.

"Two."

Her breath caught in her throat.

"Three. Go!" He rolled free.

She scrambled to her feet as quickly as she could. She kept her head down as he'd instructed, and by the time she'd gained solid footing, he was already in position, his back to the shooter, blocking any bullet that might strike her.

Time slowed to a trickle as they moved toward the opening in the rail. Each step an agony to take. The boat's engine slowed. She picked up speed and tensed for the shot she knew was coming. A bullet on the way. Not for her, but for Derrick. She wouldn't let that happen. A foot from the edge, she grabbed his hand and plunged over the side, taking him with her.

Instead of balking, he held tight to her hand, and they hit the water together as she heard another bullet pierce the railing above.

The chilly water slapped her in the face. The force knocked the breath from her body and ripped their hands apart. She couldn't get to the surface fast enough before she ran out of air. Panic settled in. She clawed for the top, her chest feeling as if it would explode if she didn't find air. She kicked harder, but her strength was failing.

Suddenly, she felt Derrick's hand grab hers and jerk her toward the surface. His strong legs carried her the last few feet to break through the water. She gasped for air, her lungs painfully expanding. Derrick came alongside her.

"That's my girl," he said as he ran his gaze over her. "Keep breathing. I'm going to wrap my arm around you and move us both under the pier."

He pulled her tightly against him and swam toward the pier using his free arm. She tried to relax and let him tow her body, but she still felt panic tightening her muscles. The boat motor, much closer now, stilled, and she knew a shot was coming.

"Grab a deep breath," Derrick said. "We're going back under."

She barely had time to take a full breath when she felt her body dragged under the water. Fear climbed up her back, and she forced herself to think of surviving for Sophia. Derrick continued swimming toward the pier and she joined him, kicking with all her might.

A bullet sliced through the surface, zipping past then slowing below them. As another one cut through the water, she forced her focus ahead to keep panic at bay. She spotted a pylon a few feet ahead and gave one final push with her legs before they surfaced again. Both of them sucked in life-giving oxygen as if it was the last they'd ever breathe.

As Derrick assessed her, her legs gave out and she was no longer able to tread water. She grabbed the pylon, slick with slime and barnacles, and held tight. He planted a hand above hers but kept treading water.

"Now what?" she asked.

"We're safe under here. I'm sure someone heard the gunshots and they called 9-1-1. We'll wait for the police to arrive."

Now that her adrenaline had started ebbing, the cold seeped in deeper—as did the realization that they'd both come within inches of losing their lives. A violent shiver started at her head and worked over her body. She felt the urge to wrap her arms around her stomach, but she couldn't let go of the piling.

"Hey." Derrick moved closer. "We're fine."

"I know, but if…" She couldn't even say the words.

He watched her carefully for a few moments, his concentration intense. He suddenly shrugged and moved even closer. Treading water with his feet only, he took her in his arms.

She knew she should move free so he didn't have to work so hard, but the strength of his arms felt so good. So safe. She relaxed into him and rested her head on his shoulder.

"You know I won't ever let anything happen to you without giving my life first, don't you?" he whispered against her ear.

She leaned her head back and looked at him. "I don't want you to give up your life for me."

"But I'd do it all the same."

What made him so willing to make the ultimate sacrifice for others? He'd done the same thing as a cop. Day in and day out, putting his life on the line for people who didn't even appreciate his sacrifice. That was commitment. Something she didn't think he possessed, but he did. Just not when it came to relationships.

"What are you thinking?" he asked.

Now was not the time to talk about his lack of commitment to her, but to celebrate his strong points. "That you're an amazing man, and I'm lucky you're so dedicated to protecting others."

A shy, crooked smile lifted the side of his mouth. "It's just what I do."

She returned his smile. "At the moment, I'm very thankful that you do."

"And I'm…" he said then shook his head. He met her gaze, his digging deep for something she couldn't name. He shifted, holding her with one arm and using the other hand to move her wet hair from her face.

"I know I shouldn't," he said. "But I have to."

"Shouldn't—" Her words were silenced by his mouth settling over hers.

This kiss was nothing like the quick little peck on the pier. This one was filled with emotions. Filled with their past feelings for each other and—if she was honest—current feelings, as well.

Her mind screamed to pull back. Especially if Kat was right and Derrick had confused his need to protect her with feelings for her.

Yet instead of heeding her own warning, she twined her arms around his neck and drew him closer. No man had ever kissed her like Derrick. This felt so right. So perfect, just as it had back in college. As if this was meant to be and God brought them together again just so they could discover they were perfect for each other.

Sirens sounded from above, ending her foray into a fantasy that could never be. The police would soon be here and this moment would be over. Needed to be over, for good. For both of their sakes.

She pulled back and squirmed out of his arms to cling to the pylon again. He watched her, not saying a word. She'd done exactly what Kat had warned her not to do. She'd led him on.

True, the stress of nearly losing her life had made her react, but there'd be no more weakness on her part. No more kissing. No more of anything between them except professional courtesy. She just couldn't risk her heart again only to lose it.

Squatting next to Gina on the pier, Derrick watched her every move. He hadn't taken his eyes off her since she'd pulled back from his kiss. Since then, the police had lifted her from the water and wrapped her in a blanket. He needed to know if she was okay. He also needed to know if the kiss meant as much to her as it did to him. He was almost glad to admit he still had feelings for her. It gave him a reason to want to finally discover the cause of his commitment phobia.

Gina shivered, and her tight expression was devoid of the joy he'd felt in her kiss.

Was it because of the police streaming on to the scene, or had she confused the joy of surviving with caring for him? He had to know, but crime scene techs scrambled around them removing slugs, and this was a private discussion.

The lanky detective who'd introduced himself as Detective Vincent when he'd arrived approached them. His heavy shoes thumped hard on the wooden pier. Derrick and Gina rose to meet him. She wobbled and he reached out to steady her, but she stepped back as if his touch might burn her.

*Great. We're back to being near strangers.*

"The salesman gave me his version of the incident." Vincent tipped his head at Zeb standing by the showroom door. "He said you wanted to purchase a boat and someone started shooting at you. Not something that happens to your average married couple."

"We're not married," Derrick said.

Vincent pulled a small notepad from his pocket but kept his focus on Derrick. "But you're buying a boat together?"

Derrick shook his head and decided to make light of the situation to alleviate the tension. "I can barely keep a goldfish alive, so owning a boat with someone is way too big of a commitment for me."

Vincent chuckled, but Gina drew in a sharp breath. Derrick took one look at the disappointment in her eyes and knew his comment had trivialized her feelings about his commitment issues. He needed to talk with her about it. Explain himself and make everything right.

"I hear ya, man," Vincent said. "The job doesn't leave me much time for anything either."

"I was a detective in Portland for six years, so I get that. Now I work with my siblings in private investigations. That's really why we're here." He explained the long saga of Gina's situation, including the other detectives' reaction to Gina's attack and Sophia's near abduction. "There're plenty of witnesses who can corroborate our story about today's attack, so I hope you won't blow this off like the others did."

"Can't speak for my fellow detectives, but whenever shots are fired, it gets my undivided attention." He tapped the pen on his notepad. "Why don't you give me a description of the shooter so we can put out an alert?"

"I only caught a glimpse, but size and build say it's a man. Tall, maybe six-two. Say one eighty or one ninety. The same size as Gina's previous attacker. He wore a dark jacket and a ski mask, so I can't give you much else."

"What about the boat?" Vincent asked. "Either of you catch a description?"

"Not other than it being loud and powerful," Gina said.

"I didn't either. Maybe Zeb got a better look at it."

Vincent smiled slyly. "He gave me a complete description down to the make and model."

"Care to share Zeb's description?" Derrick asked, though it wasn't really a question. "Before you say it goes against protocol, you know if you don't tell me, I'll just go over there and ask him."

"Former cops are the hardest people to interview." Shaking his head, Vincent flipped through his notebook and described the boat.

"Quentin's boat," Gina mumbled.

"Come again?" Vincent said.

"We're looking into a suspect who owns a boat exactly like the one you described." Derrick shared Quentin's role in the investigation.

"Not that we have any proof he's done anything wrong," Gina jumped in.

How could she keep believing in Quentin?

Derrick swung his head to look at her. "Nor do we have proof he hasn't."

"So which is it?" Vincent asked. "You think he's the guy or not?"

"He's a good friend, and I'm having a hard time believing he's responsible." Gina bit her lip and nervously looked around. "But I think he keeps his boat at this marina, so maybe it *was* him."

"And you're just now telling me that?" Derrick flashed Gina an irritated look, but the irritation was aimed mostly at himself for not checking to see if Quentin had an ongoing connection to the marina before coming here.

She tugged the blanket tighter. "I've only been on his boat once, so I'm not positive."

Derrick faced Vincent. "If he does moor his boat here, you can talk to him before he destroys any evidence."

Vincent closed his notebook. "Without a search warrant—which you know we have no chance of getting at this stage in the investigation—the best I can do is send an officer over there to keep an eye on him. If he's on the boat, we'll encourage him to let us look around."

He shouted for a nearby uniform to join them and tasked him with getting the location for Quentin's boat from Zeb and keeping an eye on Quentin.

Though this was helpful, it wasn't enough. "I'm not encumbered by your rules, so the minute you're finished with us, I'll talk to Quentin."

Vincent stepped into Derrick's path. "If he is indeed the shooter, I don't recommend that. You especially don't want to bring the little lady over there."

"Appreciate the warning. I'd have given the same one when I was on the force—but it's not going to stop me." Derrick fisted his hands.

"Derrick," Gina said softly. "I don't want to stay here without you, but if it's not safe for me to go with you…"

He gave her a comforting smile. "Quentin won't attempt anything in front of the police officer Vincent just dispatched, and he's more apt to talk with you there." Derrick turned back to Vincent. "Now, if you're finished with us, I'd like to get going."

"I should detain you just to keep you out of trouble.

Derrick stood to his full height and eyed Vincent.

"Fine." Vincent held up his hand. "I get that you have a job to do and I won't be able to stop you for long. So get out of here before I change my mind."

"Let's go talk to Quentin." Derrick pressed a hand on Gina's back and started her moving forward.

Gina dragged her feet. "But you don't know for sure that Quentin keeps his boat here."

"I'm sure Zeb will tell us." He marched down the pier a bit faster than was comfortable for Gina after the incident, but he wasn't about to let Vincent change his mind and stop them from confronting the man who'd tried to end both of their lives.

# FOURTEEN

Derrick breathed deeply to keep his anger in check. He'd had enough of this unknown foe taking shots at Gina on his watch. If Quentin truly was guilty, Derrick planned to drag a confession out of him if necessary. He parked close to Quentin's boat slip and spotted Quentin polishing the sleek exterior of his boat while the officer talked to him. With Gina's close connection to Quentin, Derrick had hoped not to find Quentin here, but the evidence spoke for itself.

Derrick lowered the binoculars and looked over the seatback. "Quentin's on his boat and the officer is with him, so it's safe for you to go with me."

She sat up and appraised him. "Maybe I should stay in the car."

Derrick wondered where the trust she'd declared earlier had gone.

*Likely disappeared after you kissed her and then made the dumb goldfish comment.*

*Great.* He'd blown things with her again. Made him even madder.

"Is there a reason you don't want to talk to him?"

She sat for a moment, her fingernail worrying over a callus. "I guess I'm afraid we'll find out that he's the one. I've lost so many people I care about lately, I'd hate to add him to that list."

Derrick felt like a jerk for being terse with her, so he tried to soften his tone. "If you're right and Quentin's innocent, then your best way to help him is to get him to tell us the truth."

"You're right." She reached for the door handle.

"Hold on. Let me make one more check of the area before you get out." He jerked open his door and made a complete circle then leaned back into the car. "You know the drill. Stay close. No stopping."

She didn't slip under his arm as readily as she had earlier, so he pulled her close. Each step with her body stiff and unresponsive next to him ate at him, and he felt his ire rising.

*Keep your cool with Gina and direct it at Quentin where it belongs.*

The officer eyed them warily, but Derrick wasn't going to let anyone stop him from getting answers out of Quentin.

"What brings the two of you down here?" Quentin asked as he set down his polishing cloth. "Especially looking like drowned rats." He chuckled.

*Laughing when Gina almost died. How dare he make light of nearly killing her.*

Derrick's anger spiraled up, fast and furious. He

planted his feet on the gently swaying boat and glared
at Quentin. "Like you don't know why we're here."

Quentin jerked his head at the police officer.
"Guess maybe you're here for the same reason as
Officer Brown."

Though Brown must recognize them from the boat
dealership, Derrick introduced himself, making sure
to tell Brown he was a former cop before turning
back to Quentin. "Are you going to let Officer Brown
search the boat?"

Quentin came to his full height, his eyes narrow-
ing. "Last I heard this's a free country, and I've done
nothing wrong, so no, I'm not."

Derrick surveyed the boat, looking for the rifle.
Found none, but Quentin was smart enough not to
leave it in plain view. He might have even tossed i
overboard. "Where is it?"

"Where's what?"

"The rifle you used to nearly kill us."

"Nearly kill you?" Quentin looked at Gina. "Are
you all right?"

She nodded.

"Do you really think I took a shot at you?"

Derrick let Gina go and stepped in front of her. "
know you did."

Derrick waited for another denial, but Quentin
didn't offer one. Derrick had interrogated enough
suspects over the years to know Quentin was care
fully weighing his response before speaking. Likely
coming up with an excuse or a fake alibi.

"Don't answer. I'll find the proof myself." Derrick started around the boat, lifting cushions to access storage in the seats.

"Aren't you going to stop him?" Quentin asked Brown, who shrugged. This was the advantage of no longer being a cop—Derrick wasn't required to provide a search warrant first.

Quentin grabbed Derrick's arm and spun him around. "My boat, my things."

Derrick jerked free. "Really?" Derrick stabbed a finger in Quentin's chest. "You really want to play it this way?"

"I'm not playing anything." Quentin knocked Derrick's finger away and widened his stance.

Derrick had had enough of this guy's attitude. With Gina's life on the line, the time for talking was over—it was time to take action. Derrick grabbed Quentin's T-shirt and slammed him up against the steering wheel. He was twenty pounds heavier and battled back, trying to dislodge Derrick, who planted his arm across Quentin's chest, pinning him in place. "We can do this the easy way or the hard way."

"Hard?" A mocking smile slowly unfolded on Quentin's face. "You don't know hard until you've trained for the CG tactical team. You couldn't even begin to dish out anything to compete."

*He's taunting me. Tempting me.*

Derrick saw red and pulled back his fist to erase Quentin's sneering smile.

"Do something!" Gina cried out to the police officer.

"They're grown men," Brown said.

"Wait." Gina grabbed Derrick's arm and pulled it back. "Quentin's right. I know what they went through in training. If Quentin doesn't want to answer, he won't. No matter what you do. So there's no point in hurting him."

The warmth of her hand cut through his rage, and Derrick sucked in a deep breath to regain control. His chest heaved as much as his brain. He'd disappointed Gina too many times already, but he still wanted to clobber Quentin.

"Please, Derrick, don't." Gina forced his fist open then wove her fingers with his.

He glanced at her, and the disappointment staring back at him cleared some of his rage. Her approval meant too much to him—he couldn't go against her wishes. He released Quentin and stepped back.

He expected Quentin to smirk, but he simply watched Derrick, as if waiting for Derrick to come at him again.

Anger still simmered in Derrick's gut, and for a moment he considered ignoring Gina. Ignore what he knew was the right thing to do. To find release by pummeling Quentin. He forced himself to take another step back, but he wouldn't let Quentin off the hook. "This isn't over."

"I don't expect it is," Quentin said calmly. Too calmly.

Gina released Derrick's hand and approached her friend. "Please don't be this way, Quentin. I don't really think you did this, but I do believe you know something you're not telling us."

He fisted his hands and stared over her head.

"It's time to stop believing in him," Derrick said. "Can't you see he's hiding his guilt?"

Gina tugged on Quentin's shirtsleeve. "If you're innocent, say something to clear your name."

Quentin didn't respond.

Derrick gently cupped his hand around Gina's elbow. "Come on. Let's get out of here."

She took one last look at Quentin and moved with Derrick to the side of the boat.

"Keep your eye on him," Derrick told Brown. "He's not to be trusted, and he'll no doubt try to destroy any evidence of his guilt."

Derrick marched them to his car and jerked open the passenger door. After settling Gina inside, he got behind the wheel and grabbed his binoculars to make sure Brown stayed put.

Derrick felt Gina's eyes on him. Was she waiting for him to erupt again? Maybe yell at her, too?

He glanced at her, found a bewildered look on her face and knew he had to apologize for losing his cool. "There's no excuse for my behavior back there. I'm sorry for the way I acted."

"I've never seen you that angry," she said, her wary expression not wavering. "Do you want to talk about it?"

Not knowing where to start, he gazed through the binoculars again. He'd behaved like an adolescent schoolboy picking a fight on the playground. Why this? Why now, when he'd always been able to control his anger in the past?

*Not always.*

He'd reacted this way two other times. Times he'd never discussed with anyone. Not even Dani. Could he tell Gina? He met her gaze, and she squeezed her eyes shut as if she was so upset with him, she didn't want to look at him. If he wanted to restore the peace between them, he'd have to tell her about his past.

"It's only happened twice before," he said, and her eyes opened. "The first time was when my parents died in the car crash. I put a fist through the wall that day."

"That's understandable." Her gentle tone washed over him. "You were just a boy and angry at the world for losing them."

"Not the world exactly," he said hesitantly. "At myself."

She leaned closer. "Yourself? Why?"

"It was my fault they were in the car." The memory assaulted him, and he looked away. "I'd gotten a new gaming system, and instead of doing my homework like I was supposed to do, night after night I played games. So my grades slipped and my teacher called my parents in for a conference. The crash happened on their way to school for the meeting."

She arched a brow. "So you think if you'd kept your grades up, they'd be alive."

He nodded. "Plus I stopped them on the way out

the door to try to explain my grades. I was the reason they didn't leave when they'd planned."

She watched him for a long moment. "You mentioned there was another time."

"The day my adoptive parents were murdered I nearly punched Ethan in the face when he told me about it. It was my fault, you see. My parents were supposed to join me for lunch. But I ran long interviewing a suspect and canceled at the last minute. If I'd stuck to the schedule, they would've been with me at the restaurant instead of home."

Her eyes opened wide. "So that's why being on time is so important to you."

He nodded again. "It probably doesn't make sense to you, but it helps me cope."

"I get it, I'm just not sure I agree with your logic," she said. "You can't blame yourself for either of those events."

"You weren't there. You don't know."

"I didn't have to be there to know a million other factors went into what happened—factors resulting from other peoples' choices that were completely out of your control. Maybe your parents could've stayed and talked to you instead of leaving. Maybe your adoptive parents would've canceled that day if you hadn't done so." She laid her hand on his arm. "I could go on and on, and each little thing could've changed the course of those days."

"But I could've changed it, too."

"Sure you could have." She slid her hand down

to his fingers and wove them with hers. "But for all we know, the end result would have been the same. We can examine the past all we want, but we can't change it." She fell silent and carefully watched him with narrowed eyes that seemed to dig to his core. "Do you really believe you're responsible for their deaths, or is it easier to blame yourself to avoid dealing with their loss?"

"What?" He jerked his hand free. "They've been gone for years. I've dealt with it."

"Really?" She raised an eyebrow. "I thought the same thing about my problems with my dad. That I left them all behind when I moved out. But you saw how I was in college and know it wasn't true." She paused and took a deep breath. "And like I mentioned the other day, it wasn't just that I hadn't dealt with it—I actually blamed myself for his behavior."

He shook his head. "I get that's what happened to you, but this is different."

"Is it?" Her tone was filled with sadness. "Is it really, or are you using this to keep from loving someone else and running the risk of losing them?"

He shrugged as his thoughts scrambled to process her comments. Was she right? Was he taking blame to avoid getting hurt again?

Gina woke from a much-needed nap and stretched pleased that her muscles were still loose from the long soak she'd had in the tub. She checked the clock and discovered she'd slept for five hours. The bath coupled with the ebbing of adrenaline from the attack must have made her conk out. She checked on Sophia and found her peacefully sleeping in her crib, so she went in search of the Justices to thank them for taking excellent care of Sophia.

She heard Derrick's voice coming from the dining room, sparking the memory of his lips warm on hers, and her feet faltered. She remembered feeling utterly content when they'd kissed. Remembered the way he'd returned her kiss with equal affection.

She'd resolved to remain detached, and yet she'd opened her heart to possibilities. And if their conversation in the car foretold the future, she was in for a world of hurt again. Once her attacker was apprehended, she'd move back to her old life and move forward alone.

Her chest ached as she continued down the hallway. She found Derrick seated at the table with Kat and Dani. Their laptops were open in front of them.

Derrick looked up and smiled. "Hey, sleepyhead. Welcome back."

"I guess the bath warmed you up and helped you relax," Dani said.

Gina forced herself to ignore Derrick's inviting smile and looked at Dani. "Sophia hasn't been sleeping all this time, has she?"

Dani held up the monitor. "I grabbed her the minute I heard her make a peep so you could get some rest."

"Thank you." Gina smiled, but Dani had already

become engrossed in her computer and didn't seem to notice. "So what are you working on?"

Dani tapped a small metal box attached by a cable to her laptop. "I'm still trying to recover files from Jon's hard drive."

"Kat and I are working on a lead Ethan gave us." Derrick leaned his chair back on two legs. "He said Quentin's uncle died recently. Though there aren't any records of the uncle leaving money to Quentin, we're trying to figure out if that's where Quentin got the cash for his boat."

"So that means he could've gotten the money from a legitimate source." A spark of happiness lit in her heart over his potential innocence.

"Not exactly," Kat said, turning her attention back to the computer. "His uncle was a known criminal."

"Quentin's uncle? A criminal?" Gina looked over Derrick's shoulder at the story open on his computer. A bold headline proclaimed the arrest of his uncle for mob-related crimes.

"So far we haven't found a connection from the uncle to Jon or Perry," Kat said.

"But you think there is one?" Gina asked, hoping this was somehow a mistake.

Derrick nodded. "It's a stretch, but it would explain why Quentin has been unwilling to tell us anything."

Gina opened her mouth to respond when Dani shot a hand into the air. "At last! I've found another email from Quentin."

"About his uncle?" Gina asked.

"No." Dani swiveled her computer. "Check it out."

Gina read the message, and a heavy feeling settled in her stomach. "I don't get it. They mention two cases where suspected killers were released because the ballistics tests didn't match their guns. What could that have to do with Jon?"

"This." Dani clicked open an internet tab to reveal that both men were known members of Renato Ontiveros's gang.

"That's the drug lord they arrested for killing Perry," Kat said, trepidation slowing her words.

A sudden coldness iced Gina's core. "And you think this is related to Jon's death?"

"Yes." Dani looked Gina directly in the eye. "Maybe Jon found out that Perry's case was dismissed due to a ballistics issue, too."

"A third ballistics issue would be an unbelievable coincidence." Derrick abruptly stood and started pacing. "Even two dismissals would be odd. But three? Impossible…unless someone tampered with the evidence."

"If Jon discovered this, Ontiveros would want to stop him before he told anyone." A grave expression crossed Kat's face, upping Gina's anxiety.

Gina felt a heaviness in her body that she couldn't shake. "If Ontiveros is really Jon's killer and now he's after me, how on earth are we going to stop him?"

No one spoke. No one had to. The unnatural stillness in the room told her they had a miniscule chance of finding and stopping Ontiveros before he succeeded in killing her.

# FIFTEEN

The next morning, Derrick disconnected his call with Ethan and went to the family room, where he'd left Gina playing on the floor with Sophia. When he walked into the room, Sophia looked up, gave him a big grin and held out her arms.

Instead of picking her up, he joined them on the floor. She crawled toward him, her little face screwed up in concentration as if he were the biggest goal she could attain. He'd never imagined the amount of joy a child could bring, but as she plopped her chubby hands on his legs and grinned up at him, he realized how important she'd become to him, and his heart squeezed out the anxiety that had lingered since the ballistics discovery last night.

He grabbed her up and hugged her, before she pushed back. Intense emotions flooded him, catching him off guard at first, but then why should he be surprised? He wanted a family. But a ready-made one? He couldn't promise to be here for Gina, much less this little munchkin. She deserved a father who'd be present for all of the important events in life. Like the first day of school. Her first date. Graduation. Marriage.

She clutched his thumbs and balanced precariously on her feet, playing with letting go for a second and then grabbing hold again. He looked up to see if Gina saw Sophia's attempt to stand on her own, but she was silently watching him, a frown on her face.

"Is something wrong?" he asked.

She shook her head, but the pensive expression didn't leave. "Was the call from Ethan something I need to know about?"

*Ah, a not-so-subtle change of subject.* She was unhappy about something, but she didn't want to share it, turning her attention to Sophia, who'd climbed down and crawled toward the fireplace.

"The call?" she asked as she redirected Sophia.

"He found receipts that show Quentin bought gas for his boat in California when you were attacked in Portland."

"Did you hear that, Soph?" Gina tickled Sophia. "Quentin's been cleared of wrongdoing."

"Before you get too excited," Derrick warned, "someone else could've used his credit card and his boat to throw us off Quentin's trail. We can't prove he was on the boat without his complete cooperation, and you know how he's been. And even if he was on the boat, he could've hired someone else to attack you."

"Maybe we should give him another chance to talk

to us. If we knew for sure he wasn't involved, we could put our full attention on finding proof against Ontiveros."

Derrick would rather not acknowledge that Ontiveros was looking more and more like the man they sought, but she was right. "How would you suggest we get Quentin to talk?"

"Maybe we can tell him what we learned about Ontiveros so he knows that the man after me is ruthless and has an army of men to do his bidding. He's wanted by multiple law enforcement agencies for so many charges that he has nothing to lose by killing me. If Quentin's a true friend, I don't see how he could refuse to cooperate with us."

Derrick wished he could embrace the same optimism, but his experience said it was unlikely. "I've seen too much over the years to hope for happily ever after endings like that."

Her focus zeroed in on him. "Just in this case or in your own life?"

He shrugged it off and picked up Sophia in hopes of redirecting Gina's focus.

"Go ahead," she said, a stony expression taking over her face. "Avoid the question like you've avoided everything else we've talked about these past few days. But at least be honest with yourself and acknowledge there's a reason you're avoiding it."

Sophia snuggled against him and rested her head on his chest. "Trust me. I'm not avoiding anything.

Since our talk yesterday, my mind's been running nonstop over how to better deal with my past."

Gina gave a slow, disbelieving shake of her head. "So what you're avoiding then is talking to me about it."

"Fine, you want to hear it?" he snapped. "I'm starting to think that things—important things—in my life are beyond my control. Despite my best efforts, things go south regardless of what I do to stop it."

She watched him with such intensity that he had to look away. "So you're willing to forgo all that you want in life never to let that happen again?"

Was he?

He peered at Sophia, her thumb in her mouth as her eyes fluttered closed. Even with the turmoil surrounding him, holding her filled him with complete and utter contentment. He thought of Ethan with his son and Cole with his adopted twins. Birth child or adopted, the love they both exhibited was well beyond anything Derrick had been able to comprehend in the past. But now? Here with Sophia—with Gina—he got it. Really got it.

Question was, would he find a way to deal with his past, or was he willing to give up this kind of feeling for life? He just didn't know, and that made him sadder than he thought possible.

Gina and Derrick hurried toward Quentin's apartment, but Gina's mind wasn't on Quentin. Derrick had insisted he needed her to run interference after yesterday's altercation. But how could she help when she couldn't concentrate after his admission? An admission made with Sophia snuggled against his chest.

Gina had failed Sophia. She'd let Derrick spend too much time with her and she'd bonded with him. Now her precious niece was going to miss him when the case ended, and that wasn't fair to her. Gina resolved to limit their time together so the connection didn't grow any further.

He tightened his hold, reminding her of how much she'd let go of her self-reliance and come to depend on him for support, too. But he wasn't the staying-around kind of guy. Maybe Gina needed to take her own advice and let go of her past for Sophia. She deserved a father. One who believed life was filled with promise and hope. Not a man like Derrick, who didn't believe in happily ever afters.

He released his hold at Quentin's door and looked at her. "I'd like you to take the lead on this, and I'll hang in the background."

She nodded her agreement, and he knocked. She soon heard heavy footsteps thumping their way.

Quentin opened the door, and his eyes immediately narrowed. "I thought we'd hashed everything out yesterday."

Gina rested her hand on his arm. "Can we talk one more time? Just for a minute."

"The kids are home, so it'll have to be out here."

"That's fine." Gina stepped back.

Quentin pulled the door closed and scowled at Derrick.

Derrick lifted his hands and backed away. "Don't worry. I'm on my best behavior today."

A hint of a smile settled on Quentin's lips. Gina was certain if he was guilty he wouldn't smile.

Derrick tipped his head at an alcove housing a trash chute and recycle station. "Let's step over here to minimize any danger to Gina."

Gina focused on Quentin. "We've had a break in the case. I thought you should hear about the man we think is trying to kill me."

Quentin appraised her. "So I'm not your prime suspect anymore?"

"You're not off the hook yet," Derrick warned. "But someone else has come to our attention."

Gina launched into Ontiveros's story, making sure Quentin knew the danger Ontiveros posed. "We have an uphill battle to stop him, and I'm hoping you'll finally agree to help us."

Quentin rubbed his hand over his head and seemed to war with a decision. "I'm so sorry. I hate that this creep is after you, and you know I'll do everything I can to keep him away from you."

"Is that so?" Derrick crossed his arms. "Then why have you been stonewalling us?"

Quentin firmed his jaw. "I was under direct orders not to talk."

"I don't understand," Gina said.

"It all started when Perry died. When the ballistics for Ontiveros's gun, or any of the other guns confiscated in the raid, failed to match the slug recovered from Perry's body, Jon thought Ontiveros had pulled a fast one."

"So this *is* about Perry, then," Gina said.

Quentin nodded. "At least, I'm pretty sure it is now that you tell me Ontiveros is involved in the attempts on your life."

"But how could this possibly relate to me?"

"Jon couldn't let Perry's death go. The official report said Perry's shooter must've been one of Ontiveros's goons who fell overboard after he was shot. The raid happened at sea, so they didn't recover a body or gun. Jon was the team leader and felt guilty for Perry's death. Though he thought he'd seen Ontiveros fire the fatal shot, the scene was so chaotic that his testimony on that point wasn't given much weight. So he started investigating on his own. I thought it was pointless until he found two other cases involving ballistics and Ontiveros's men."

"When was that?" Derrick asked.

"The afternoon he crashed. He called me and said he'd received a log that proved Perry's case wasn't as clear-cut as we'd believed. He said he'd show the log to me when he got home."

"But he didn't get home," Derrick added.

"You knew about the log?" Gina let her disappointment flow through her words. "How could you keep that from me?"

Quentin flinched, but she didn't care. She felt betrayed.

"I knew *about* the log, but I've never seen it, so I couldn't help you."

"Same difference," Derrick said.

"Maybe, but like I said, I was under direct orders not to talk about it."

"Why would someone order you to stay quiet on a closed case?" Derrick asked.

"After Jon's death, I convinced my supervisor to reopen Perry's case. But he didn't want anyone else to know. He feared if word got out, it would distract the team and put them in danger on raids. And he also worried that Ontiveros would get wind of it and flee before he was apprehended." Quentin made eye contact with Gina. "I'm sorry, Gina, but you know how it goes when a commanding officer puts a gag order on something. I have to obey. If we don't have that discipline in the military, we don't have anything."

"I understand," Gina said, and she really did. "Jon lived by that code, and I know you have to also."

"So why are you talking now?" Derrick asked, suspicion still lodged in his voice.

"The CG investigators have given up. Said they can't find a thing to prove any wrongdoing in Perry's case, and if they couldn't find anything on Perry's shooting, there was no point in looking into Jon's accident." He shook his head sorrowfully side to side.

"Just like that. They give up on two of the finest men I've known. Two of our own. I want you to find whoever killed Perry and Jon and bring them to justice. I'll help in any way I can."

Derrick cocked his head and stared at Quentin. "Sounds like a nice story. But with no proof of what you're saying, I won't rule you out as a suspect."

Quentin's nostrils flared. "I wasn't even in Portland when Gina was attacked."

"Where were you?" Gina asked calmly, hoping her tone would keep the situation from escalating between the two men.

"I'd tracked down a lead on Ontiveros. I took my boat and followed up on it."

"Any proof of that?" Derrick demanded.

"Right here in my wallet." Quentin dug in his back pocket, while Derrick watched Quentin's every move.

Gina winced at the ferocity in Derrick's eyes. Hoping Derrick would remember her pleas from yesterday, she stepped closer to him and caught his attention. She took a deep breath and slowly blew it out. He caught on and did the same thing, making him visibly relax.

"Here." Quentin pulled receipts from his wallet and shoved them at Derrick. "I bought gas at a few stops."

Derrick held up his hand. "We've already seen the charges on your credit card. All they prove is that your card was used to buy gas, not that you used it."

Quentin fired a testy look at Derrick. "I understand how much you want to help Gina, so I'll ignore the fact that you dug into my finances without authorization."

"Are you trying to avoid the question?" Derrick challenged.

"No. I stayed at a marina overnight." Quentin offered the name of the marina and the owner's name. "I talked with the owner about his son who's in the Coast Guard, so I'm sure he'll remember me."

Derrick pulled out a notepad and jotted down the information. "I'll follow up, but it doesn't rule out the possibility that you hired someone to go after Gina."

"If I paid someone, there would be a financial trail. You've dug into my credit cards, so I'm sure you've looked at the rest of my finances, too."

"You could have hid it. After all, there's no transaction history for the purchase of your boat."

"Got the money from my uncle." Quentin lifted his chin. "Before he died, he buried a box on his property and told my aunt I was to dig it up and not tell anyone about it. It was filled with cash and a letter telling me to buy the boat. They didn't have any kids, and he wanted to give me what I'd always dreamed of."

Gina blew out a frustrated breath. "Why didn't you just tell us that?"

"I should've reported it to the IRS, but then they would've confiscated the money. My uncle wanted me to buy the boat, so that's what I did." Quentin looked away. "He was involved in some pretty bad stuff. Criminal stuff. I figure he got most of his money illegally. I know I should have refused it, but I've always wanted the boat."

He paused and looked squarely at Gina, embarrassment crowning on his face. "Not that there's any good excuse, but you know how much money we make on the team. I'd never be able to afford a boat on my salary, and I'm not about to leave the Guard. So I gave in. Made a rash decision. Then I thought about what I'd done and figured if people knew where the money came from, they'd judge me. Maybe someone would report me to the IRS, and I'd go to jail. So Val and I made a pact to keep it to ourselves."

"I so hoped you weren't involved in Jon's death or the attacks against me." Gina threw her arms around Quentin's neck and gave him a quick hug. She looked up at him. "I'm sorry I ever doubted you."

"I'm not worthy of your kindness, Gina. If you need to report me for the money, go ahead. I deserve it."

"It's not up to me to report you, but I imagine you'd feel a whole lot better if you told the IRS what you did."

"I'll give it some thought," he said warily. "If you need anything else from me let me know."

"Maybe you could help us now." Gina looked at Derrick.

He shook his head.

"Why not?" she challenged.

"Because he doesn't believe me," Quentin said. "And until he does, he isn't going to let me anywhere near you."

Derrick's brow rose in surprise.

"Hey, man," Quentin said, "we may have our differences, but I'd do the same thing."

Derrick nodded.

Gina looked at him. "I don't agree with you, but I can see there's nothing I can do to change your mind." Gina gave Quentin another hug and they departed.

Derrick pulled her close and marched toward his car as if he was angry. The minute he slammed her car door, she saw him pull out his phone and dial. He slid behind the wheel and she listened from the backseat as he tasked Ethan with calling the marina to verify the alibi and double-checking Quentin's finances. He ended the call and cast an irritated look in his mirror.

"What's with the scowl?" Gina asked. "It's clear you still don't believe Quentin, so why aren't you happy to make the call just for the chance to prove him wrong?"

"Think about it," he said. "If Quentin is truly innocent, then that means Ontiveros is now our prime suspect." He lifted his eyes to the mirror. "I'd rather be hunting down just about anyone than a known killer who continually evades the law."

Phone to his ear, Derrick paced in the study at Tracy's house. Maybe he'd misunderstood Ethan.

"You're sure Quentin's telling the truth?" Derrick asked, though he knew what the answer would be.

"Sorry, man," Ethan replied. "He was at the marina

just like he said. And even after double-checking, his finances received a clean bill of health."

"Still doesn't clear him 100 percent."

"No one will be cleared 100 percent until you find the actual killer. But spending any more time on him will sidetrack you from the real suspect."

"I get it, bro," Derrick said reluctantly. "I may not like it, but I get it."

"Trust me. After the way Jennie was hunted down a few years ago, I can totally see why looking at Ontiveros as our prime suspect has you spooked." Derrick sighed, recalling the situation Ethan's wife had gone through. "Just remember everything worked out with Jennie, and it won't be any different for Gina."

A long pause filled the phone, and Derrick assumed Ethan expected him to say something. But what could he say?

"I moved the whole team to working on Ontiveros full-time," Ethan finally said. "If anything turns up, I'll let you know."

As Derrick hung up, he couldn't stop the memories of Jennie's run for her life. The killer had almost bested all of them. Ethan had been beside himself.

*Much like you're acting with Gina.*

Derrick knew it was time he admitted Gina was right. Losing his parents had made him hold back to keep from getting hurt. Now he had to find a way to get over it before Gina and Sophia walked out of his life for good.

# SIXTEEN

"The log," Dani shouted from the dining room, bringing everyone running. "I've found the log."

Gina hurried across the room. "Where'd you find it?"

Dani stabbed a finger at her computer screen. "On an online storage site. Jon must've uploaded it in case he lost the flash drive."

Gina stared at the screen. "How in the world did you know to check there?"

"I found his login for the site hidden in his computer's deleted files."

"Let me see it." Derrick barreled past Gina and studied the screen. "It looks like a police log of some sort, doesn't it?"

"Maybe an evidence log," Dani said.

Kat pushed between them and perused the screen. "I agree. Now we just have to figure out which law enforcement agency it's from."

Dani nodded. "Since Jon was investigating Perry's death—"

"It could be for the San Diego police," Derrick jumped in excitedly.

Dani pulled the computer back in front of her. "I'll try to track the numbers to see if Perry's case number is on the list."

"Shoot a copy of the log to my phone." Derrick dug his keys from his pocket. "I'll head to the police station and show it to Detective Gleason. Hopefully he can confirm it's from their department. Maybe he can also figure out if it links to the other cases with ballistics issues."

Gina stepped forward. "I suppose there's no point in asking if you'll let me go with you."

He looked at her, his eyes warm and tender, and gently took her hand. "I'd feel better if you'd stay here. Would you mind?"

"Feel better? Mind staying here?" Dani's voice climbed higher with each word. "Since when did a Justice male start acting all wishy-washy when someone's life was in danger?"

"Talk to your other brothers," Derrick said, but his eyes never left Gina. "They've been this way since the day they got married." Derrick squeezed Gina's hand and then departed.

His touch lingered, as did the warmth from his gaze. She didn't know what to make of the change in him, but she knew it made her heart swell, and she struggled to contain her hopefulness as Kat and Dani both intently studied her.

"I need to check on Sophia," she said quickly then

fled the room. She peeked in the bedroom door, but as she suspected, Sophia was fast asleep. She closed the door and stood in the hallway. For the first time in a few days, she found herself with nothing to do but analyze Derrick's behavior.

*Forget about him. Get busy. Do something.*

She'd seen dishes in the sink earlier. She could take care of them and not only repay a little of Tracy's kindness but also occupy her mind. She hurried to the kitchen. Her mind continued to drift to Derrick, so she started humming a violin concerto.

"One of my favorites," Kat said from behind her, making Gina jump.

"You scared me."

"Sorry. I needed more coffee." Kat lifted the coffeepot and eyed Gina. "But since we're alone, I'd like to talk to you."

Assuming Kat wanted to discuss what had just taken place with Derrick, Gina stifled a groan and forced herself to meet Kat's gaze. "If this's about Derrick again, don't worry. I haven't encouraged him *at all.*"

*Except for the kiss. The wonderful kiss that you returned wholeheartedly.* She blushed at the thought and looked down at the dishes.

"I shouldn't have warned you off like I did," Kat said, making Gina's head snap back up. "I've had a chance to get to know you better. It's clear you care about Derrick and want what's best for him."

"I'm glad you can see that," Gina responded, though she was flustered to think that her feelings were so transparent.

"He told me about your father the other night, and I can totally see why you ended things with Derrick in college."

"Okay." Gina tensed as she waited for the other shoe to drop.

Kat gripped her cup so hard her fingers turned white. "I won't understand if you lead him to believe there's a future with you and then bolt."

"Again, you have nothing to worry about. I know there's no future with Derrick."

*Then why are you still hoping for one? Especially when you have Sophia to think about?*

"You believe that's what you're conveying to him, but I see the opposite," Kat said. "You have to decide what you want. If you want to risk him not being able to commit for the chance at having a relationship again, then go all in—and be there for the long haul. If not, keep your distance."

Her comment about commitment made Gina really consider what would happen if she gave in and embraced her feelings for Derrick, but all she could see was him letting down not only her but a tearful Sophia. Gina's heart broke at the very thought. Even if she could let go of her trust issues and pursue a future with Derrick, she couldn't put Sophia at risk for disappointment. Of that, she was certain.

* * *

Seated next to Detective Gleason's desk, Derrick leaned closer. "You're sure the log is a ballistics report from your department?"

"I'm positive." Gleason handed Derrick's phone back to him.

Derrick let the news settle over him and pondered the implication. "We need to review the cases listed on the log to see what they have in common."

"We? There's no 'we' in this." Gleason eyed Derrick. "*I* fully intend to do a thorough review. *After* you leave."

Derrick didn't know what it would take to get this man to bend the rules a bit, but Derrick wouldn't let the detective shut him out. "Could you at least run the numbers through the database to let me know if Perry Axton's case is on the log?"

Without replying, Gleason turned his attention to his computer. He pecked at the keyboard with one finger then sat back. Derrick was tempted to look at the screen, but he had to give Gleason the same respect he would demand if he were in the detective's position. The screen flashed and Gleason stared at it. He suddenly hissed out a breath and gave Derrick a pointed look.

"Message received," Derrick said, knowing that the log held Perry's case number but the detective wouldn't outright confirm it.

"I may be pushing my luck here, but how about checking for two of Ontiveros's goons?" Derrick slid a piece of paper holding the names of the men who'd escaped prosecution due to ballistics discrepancies across the desk.

Gleason followed the same routine, including the hissing breath and pointed stare. Derrick resisted shooting his fist in the air at the firm connection between Ontiveros and Jon's death.

Gleason held up the paper. "What do these guys have to do with your case?"

"Each of them escaped a murder rap when ballistics for their weapons didn't match the slugs recovered from the bodies."

Gleason's eyes narrowed. "You think the tests were falsified?"

Derrick nodded. "Ontiveros could easily pay to have the reports doctored."

Gleason shook his head. "I don't buy it. He'd need a source inside our forensic science unit."

"We never want to think police department employees are susceptible to corruption," Derrick said earnestly. "But money has a way of making things happen that you'd have never imagined."

"I don't know." Gleason massaged his forehead.

"You could at least see if the same forensic tech worked on all three of these cases."

"That I can do, but don't ask me to share the tech's name with you. I won't rat out one of our own."

"I totally understand," Derrick said, though he'd hoped Gleason would bend the rules. "But you will make sure an investigation is opened, right?"

"I'll talk to my supervisor. He's a stand-up guy and he'll do the right thing." Gleason made direct eye contract. "But remember. Even if your theory proves true, the odds of bringing Ontiveros to justice are slim to none."

"You mean because he's hard to locate?" Derrick's worry over Gina's safety ratcheted up.

Gleason nodded and propped his foot on an open drawer. "If Ontiveros hears about our investigation, he's bound to go even deeper underground to avoid arrest. We'll do our best to keep it on a need-to-know basis, but if Ontiveros has someone on our payroll…" He lifted his shoulder in a quick shrug.

"You'll just have to work harder to keep it quiet, then." Derrick fired a testy look at Gleason.

"I'm not worried about a leak in our department, but we'll have to ask another agency to retest the ballistics. Any time you bring in someone from the outside, your risk of exposure goes up. You know that."

Unfortunately, Derrick *did* know that, but he didn't have to accept it. "Work faster then and keep the odds in our favor."

"Let me remind you again, Justice." Gleason's foot dropped to the floor and he leaned closer. "I'm here to do my job, not to cater to your interests. I'm a sworn officer of the law and can only work as fast as the law allows. I can't run off half-cocked like your team can. I have procedures to follow. That involves a methodical gathering of the evidence and obtaining warrants before we can even contemplate an arrest."

Derrick's anger rose over his inability to do anything. He curled his fingers into a fist. "My client could be dead by then."

"I'm sorry, man, but you know we have no probable cause to even bring Ontiveros in for questioning, much less to arrest him." Gleason sucked in a fortifying breath. "When I *can* legally obtain an arrest warrant, I will."

"There must be something else we can do." Derrick glanced around the bullpen, searching for an answer. A female officer passed by, giving him an idea. "You could put one of your female officers undercover posing as Gina to lure Ontiveros into the open."

"If I asked my supervisor for the resources to pull that off without a shred of probable cause, he'd laugh me out of his office."

"You could at least try," Derrick said, despite knowing that when he was a detective he would never have taken such a request to his supervisor.

Gleason snorted.

"Fine." Derrick stood. "All of my siblings have law enforcement backgrounds. We'll set up the sting ourselves."

"You know I can't sanction such a move." Gleason slowly came to his feet and lowered his voice. "But if I was in the position of losing someone I love and had family members trained in police procedures, I'd do the same thing."

Biting back his frustration, Derrick asked Gleason to keep him in the loop on the investigation and left the office. As he drove back to Tracy's, his idea of a sting operation started seeming less far-fetched. In fact, a decoy was the perfect way to smoke out Ontiveros. It would be dangerous, though. Not to Gina, who'd have no part in the action, but to the person they put in the decoy position. Likely Dani, as she resembled Gina more than Kat. He hated to put her in danger, but he also hated the thought of losing Gina. Besides, Dani was well trained and—as she constantly told her brothers and her husband—she was very capable of taking care of herself. He'd throw this idea out to the family for a vote.

He quickly parked and hurried up the walkway to Tracy's house. Before opening the door, he heard Sophia screaming in pain. Even her tearful cry on the airplane hadn't been this distraught.

*Are they in trouble?*

His heart thudding, he drew his weapon and eased inside. In the family room, he found Gina, clearly frazzled and walking Sophia, whose face was red and blotchy. His heart ached for the obvious pain on both of their faces. At the same time, relief for their safety flooded him.

He holstered his gun and met Gina in the middle of the room. "She okay?"

Gina shrugged. "I think she's trying to cut a tooth."

"Isn't there something that will help?"

Gina moved Sophia's sweaty hair from her forehead. "Kat will be back from the store with teething gel any minute, but I don't know if I can last that long."

He held out his hands. "Let me take her for a while."

Gina flashed a surprised look at him. He was equally surprised by his offer.

She watched him for a few moments. "You're sure?"

He nodded. "You need a break."

"Then I'm thankful for your help."

Derrick took Sophia. She studied him and her crying stilled. Maybe he had a special touch. Her face screwed up again and she wailed with renewed vigor.

Gina backed out of the room. "Let me know if she gets to be too much."

"It's okay, Bug. Let it out." He mimicked Gina's method of bouncing and walking Sophia. He really had no clue what he was doing, but he wanted to help Gina. Raising a child was such a big responsibility. He hated that Gina had to do it alone.

If only he could change his take on life. Become the man Gina wanted him to be. *Please, Father, show me exactly what it will take to get me there.*

# SEVENTEEN

Sitting on her bed with the door closed, Gina breathed in and slowly exhaled. She could still hear Sophia screaming through the solid door. Gina should never have imposed on Derrick this way—she should go back to the family room. But she was tired. So tired. A few minutes alone would help her cope with Sophia, and in the long run that would be better for her.

She set a five-minute alarm on her watch and pulled out her Bible. She tuned out Sophia and immersed herself in the words in Corinthians. One of her favorite verses spoke to her. *My grace is sufficient for you, for my power is made perfect in weakness.*

Gina leaned back and thought about what she'd gone through in the past. God's grace had brought her through it all, proving He would get her through her recent losses and these attacks, leaving her stronger for them. Strength, true strength, was gained in suffering, she remembered her pastor saying recently.

So why had she lamented the years spent with her

father? The strength she'd gained from his rejection made her a better person. A better mother to Sophia. Even when the little sweetheart was in pain and screaming uncontrollably as she was tonight. All suffering had a purpose, and as long as Gina remembered that, she'd be fine.

Resolved to take back her duties, she offered her thanks to God and opened the door. She expected to hear Sophia, but the house was silent. She tiptoed to the family room and found Derrick on the sofa, his head resting on the back, his eyes closed, and Sophia asleep on his shoulder.

The sight of the two of them melted her heart, and realization struck. She was using what she'd learned with her father to be a better mother and a better person, some of the time. But not with Derrick. She'd been so afraid of getting hurt—and of letting Sophia get hurt—that she hadn't even wanted to allow Derrick to spend time with the baby. That was ridiculous when Derrick was so amazingly good with her.

She'd also let her past with her dad negatively color her relationship with Derrick in college. None of that had been fair to Derrick. If she'd truly let go of her past as she'd counseled Derrick to do, she'd follow her feelings and give him a chance to prove himself.

The thought of opening herself to pain made her take an involuntary step back. She banged into a hall table, jerking Derrick awake. When he saw her, a relaxed smile played across his mouth, reminding her of their lazy Saturday afternoons in college.

Could she really give him another chance?

She willed her heart to slow and walked over to him. "You're a wonder with Sophia."

"Nah. Kat came home with teething gel. We rubbed it on Bug's gums, and she sighed then dropped off." He smiled down on her. "Poor little thing exhausted herself."

"I can put her in her crib if you'd like."

"Are you kidding—and risk waking her?" He grinned.

Gina sat next to them. "She's really taken to you."

"I kinda like her, too." His eyes darkened. "I'll miss her."

"You should really think about having a family. You deserve happiness, and I can see a child provides you with that."

"I never expected it, but she does brighten my life. A lot. But…"

"But you still don't believe you deserve a family."

He shrugged, making Sophia stir. He gently rubbed her back.

Gina really didn't want to speak of her recent breakthrough without thinking it through, but she couldn't keep silent if it helped Derrick. "Maybe it would help if you looked at the loss of your parents as something that has helped you grow stronger, instead of letting it hold you back."

He stared at the ceiling for a long moment then met her gaze. "Sounds good in theory, but no matter how many times I've thought about my past in the last few days—and trust me, I've thought about it since the moment I saw you again—changing the way I see things is something I haven't been able to do, even with God's help."

"I'd never tell you it's easy to change." She took his free hand and threaded her fingers with his. "I'm still working on things, but I know if I hadn't spent years looking at everything through the lens of my father's rejection, I would've done so many things differently."

"Like?" he whispered.

"Like, I could've been more patient with you and given you a chance instead of walking out."

"And now? This thing between us." He lifted her hand and pressed a soft kiss on the back. "Even if I can't promise to be there forever, are you willing to give a relationship a chance?"

Was she? Was she really?

She'd been so bold, sharing her new breakthrough, but as with any newly learned life skill, she had to test and embrace it. To live it. And only time would tell if she could pull it off.

Derrick remained on the sofa, preparing for the family conference call, while Gina put Sophia to bed. She'd never answered his question but had promised they'd talk later. He didn't want to get excited about the possibilities their discussion opened, but hope flittered around his heart, teasing, taunting. A foreign feeling. He wanted to grab hold, but he found it elusive.

Dani entered the room. "I've got everyone on the conference call. Kat's getting Gina."

The reminder of his very dangerous proposal for the family sent his hope darting away.

*For now,* he told himself as he followed Dani out of the room. After Ontiveros was behind bars, Derrick would have plenty of time with Gina, but only if he was able to protect her first.

She was already sitting beside Kat at the dining table when he entered the room. Dani's laptop was open in front of them. Derrick pulled up a chair.

"So what's this big idea you have, Derrick?" Ethan asked.

Derrick recounted his meeting with the detective. "I was frustrated with Gleason and I suggested the undercover sting without thinking. On my drive home, I decided my idea has merit."

"I agree," Dani said. "With a wig and dim lights, I can easily pass for Gina. And—" she paused and held up a hand "—before any of you argue with me, remember I'm trained to handle this type of situation. Plus with Kat and Derrick at my back, I'll be fine."

"No," Gina blurted out. "I couldn't let you put yourself in danger like that. If anything happened to you, I'd never forgive myself."

"If we don't do this and anything happens to you, I'll never forgive myself either," Derrick said, filling his voice with as much vehemence as he could muster.

Gina looked at him. "That's different. I'm the one in danger. Dani's just an innocent bystander."

Dani rested her hand on Gina's. "We're committed to helping people in situations like this despite the risk. It's what we do."

"But I—"

"No *buts,* I'm doing it." Dani faced Kat. "You in?"

"Of course." Kat's ready agreement was no surprise, as his sisters always stuck together.

Dani turned back to her computer. "Everyone else on board?"

"I'm in," Cole said.

Ethan nodded. "Me, too, but we need to move quickly, before Ontiveros catches wind of the police investigation."

"I'd like to get back to Luke ASAP, so why not do this tonight? At Gina's apartment."

Derrick could hear the loneliness in his sister's tone, and he felt guilty for insisting she travel to San Diego. But if he hadn't, they wouldn't be able to implement his plan. "I appreciate your coming here more than you can know."

She playfully punched him as she had a habit of doing when he got serious. "Then let's get the show on the road."

"I won't do this without a thorough threat assessment and a foolproof plan," Derrick warned.

"Then time's a wasting." Dani clapped him on the back. "If Kat will stay here with Gina and Sophia, we can head over to Gina's apartment and scope it out."

"I'm good to stay," Kat said.

"Then it's a go." Derrick stood and looked at Gina. "We'll be back soon with a plan to end this once and for all."

Gina shot out a hand. "Wait a minute. If Ontiveros is so hard to find, how are you going to make sure he knows about this?"

"Nothing easier than getting word to a felon," Cole said.

"Cole's U.S. marshal experience makes him an expert on knowing how a criminal's thought process works," Kat explained.

"We simply need to find the right source, and the news will spread like wildfire," Cole added. "And I have the perfect person in mind to get the word out."

"Great." Derrick clapped his hands to signal an end to the meeting. "Make contact with your person, and I'll give you the green light when the plan's set."

"You got it, bro," Cole said. "Now make us proud."

Antsy to get going, Derrick shifted his feet. "Any other questions, Gina?"

"No." She stood and touched his arm. "Just be careful, okay?"

"Yeah, Derrick, be careful," Cole said in a singsong voice.

Derrick glared at the screen.

Cole stifled a smile. "Let it go, kid. You've teased all of us for the past few years about our love lives, and it's payback time."

Derrick wanted to claim there was no love life, but

if he could apprehend Gina's attacker and she saw fit to give him a chance to work through his fears, he sincerely hoped there would be.

Later that evening, Gina watched Derrick fasten his Kevlar vest before heading to her apartment to launch their undercover operation. He seemed so eager to rush in and resolve this. She hoped it was in part because he was thinking about their discussion this afternoon and was ready to embrace the things he wanted out of life.

He checked his gun then settled it in the holster. "We need to get going."

"Be careful." She tried to keep the apprehension out of her voice, but it was there, big and bold.

"Hey." He crossed over to her. "We do things like this all the time. Our plan is solid, and we'll be back before you know it."

"I know."

He studied her so intently that a crease formed between his eyes. "We'll get through this. Together."

She didn't know if he meant tonight's event or their future. Either way, she didn't want him to be concerned for her when his mind needed to be on his assignment, so she didn't ask.

"I'll be fine," she said, her eyes riveted to his. She felt like she needed to memorize them in case something happened to him.

A surge of heat sparked between them. His hand captured hers, and he pressed a kiss to her palm.

"Tracy's in charge here, and I'll call you the minute Ontiveros is in custody."

"Thank you." She clung to his hand. "For everything you've done. I can never repay you or your family."

He put a finger to her lips, silencing her. "No repayment needed."

Dani stepped to the doorway and lingered in the hall shadows. She looked so much like Gina that she had to do a double take as she let go of Derrick's hand.

"I guess your look says I pass." Dani entered the room, the similarity evaporating in the bright light.

"It's uncanny," Gina agreed.

Dani fluffed her wig and winked, making Gina laugh. "Kat's already in the car. Are you ready, bro?"

He nodded and smiled at Gina. "I'll call you as soon as I know anything."

Gina watched them go. The room suddenly felt lifeless and unsettling as worry for Derrick, Kat and Dani filled her mind. Derrick had said the operation could take hours. She'd go crazy if she sat here and let worry take over. She went in search of Tracy and found her in her study curled in a club chair, a book on her lap.

Gina knocked on the door. "Mind if I stay with you until they come back?"

"Grab a book and settle in." Tracy gestured at her extensive library.

After browsing for a while, Gina pulled out a random book and tried to read, but the ticking of the mantel clock kept reminding her that time was passing so slowly while Derrick and his sisters were endangering their lives for her.

*Tick. Tick. Tick.* The sound made every second unbearable. She had to move. Do something. Be busy. She got up and put the book back.

"Done so soon?" Tracy asked.

"I can't concentrate," Gina replied. "I'll just check on Sophia."

She marched down the hall without a clue what she would do after she made sure Sophia was sleeping. Maybe she could offer to dust or vacuum the already spotless house.

Sophia was asleep as Gina had expected. She'd gone down for the night effortlessly, so Gina doubted the teething pain would wake her again. Gina wandered back down the hallway.

A loud thump came from the library. It sounded like something hitting the floor.

"Is everything okay, Tracy?" Gina called as she hurried toward the room. "Did you hear that noise?" When Tracy didn't respond, Gina picked up speed.

A hand came over her mouth as the barrel of a gun was jammed into her temple.

Gina tried to scream, but the hand clamped tighter. Her heart thumped so hard, she felt as if it was trying to escape her chest. She tried another scream, but her muffled sounds traveled nowhere.

"There's no point in screaming," said a rumbling

male voice. "Your friend is out and you'll just wake your kid. Then I'd have to take her with us."

*Sophia, no! I can't risk him hurting Sophia.*

He cocked the gun and ground the icy barrel into her temple. "If you don't want me to use this, you'll do exactly as I say."

As his minty breath fanned over her neck, she pondered his voice. No hint of an accent. Ontiveros was from Mexico. Was it him or one of his goons? Did he somehow know they'd planned to trap him?

"If you promise not to yell again, I'll take my hand off your mouth. Nod if you agree."

She nodded quickly.

He dropped his hand, and she gulped in air.

"Slowly now. Put your hands behind your back," he commanded as if he was used to being obeyed. Exactly the way Ontiveros would act. If it was him, she had no choice but to do as he said. He wouldn't hesitate to kill her.

Maybe Sophia, as well.

As she complied with his demand, she couldn't seem to take in enough oxygen.

*Breathe. Just breathe. In and out. Slowly. In. Out. That's it. Think about anything else but the cuffs he's clamping around your wrists.*

*Tracy.* "What did you do to Tracy?"

He chuckled. "A little conk on the head. She'll wake up embarrassed at failing to protect you and with a monster headache, but she'll be fine."

*Will I wake up tomorrow? If not, who will care for Sophia?*

"Please don't hurt me," she pleaded.

"If you follow my directions, you'll be fine." He secured the handcuff on her second wrist. "We're going for a little drive." He spun her around.

She expected to see a man with Hispanic origins, but this guy was white and pasty. "Who are you?"

He laughed. "Not who you expected, huh?"

"Did Ontiveros send you to get me? Are you taking me to him?"

"You'll know soon enough. Now move." He clamped a hand on her shoulder and shoved her toward the back door.

She winced at the intensity of his grip as she looked for something, anything, she could leave behind to tell Derrick where she was. But as he dragged her out the door, the only thing she could do was pray that Derrick would find her before this creep delivered her to Ontiveros and the ruthless killer ended her life.

# EIGHTEEN

Something wasn't right.

Derrick checked his watch in the gloom of Gina's hall closet. They'd been in place—Dani in the family room and Kat in the bedroom—for two hours now with no action.

None.

Even if Ontiveros didn't make an appearance, Derrick had expected one of his goons to show up. Cole worked the situation perfectly. He'd made it easy enough for Ontiveros to get wind of their plan, but not too easy to spook him.

Derrick's phone vibrated in his pocket. He cupped his hand over the already darkened screen and found Tracy's icon blinking at him.

*Gina.* His gut twisted as he pressed the icon.

"Tracy," he whispered.

"He knocked me out." She sounded out of breath. "Took Gina."

Derrick's breath left his body, and he struggled to pull in another one.

*Calm down. You can't help Gina like this.*

"When?" he croaked out the word.

"I don't know. Could've been a while. I've been out cold."

"What about Sophia? Is Sophia okay?" He tensed as he waited for the answer.

"He didn't touch her. She's fine."

*Thank You, Father. Keep Gina safe, too. Help me find her.*

How? Thoughts ran across Derrick's mind like a ticker tape. What should he do first?

*Think, man, think. This is your job. Investigation 101. Run the steps.*

Process the scene of Gina's abduction. Follow up the leads. Get the family involved.

He shot out of the closet. "Are you good to process the scene, Tracy?"

"Yes."

"Get started then and call in help if you can. We'll run the rescue mission from here. Call me as soon as you have even the smallest lead." He hung up and yelled for his sisters.

They both came running. Dani reached him first. She took one look at him and grabbed his arm. "What's wrong? Who's hurt?"

"Someone knocked Tracy out and abducted Gina."

"Oh, no." Dani's hand fell limp to her side.

Kat stepped forward. "How long ago?"

"We don't know. Tracy's been unconscious, so she has no idea how much of a head start they have."

Kat's eyes narrowed. "I hate to say this, but if Ontiveros has her, he could've gone deep underground by now."

*And finding Gina alive will be next to impossible,* Derrick thought. He felt as if an elephant sat on his chest. "I should've known not to leave her."

"Hey, you can't blame yourself for this." Dani squeezed his hand and studied him. "You used the information we had at the time to make a sound decision in Gina's best interest."

"I know, but—"

"No *buts,* it's a fact," Kat said. "Don't let this distract you. We need to focus on finding her."

"She's right." Dani let go of his hand and firmed her shoulders.

"We need a lead." Kat's no-nonsense tone comforted Derrick more than any platitude might. "Let's review what we know."

He swallowed hard, biting back his worry and putting on his investigator's hat. "We know that Ontiveros is behind all of this. And we know he didn't act alone in the cover-up."

"Good," Kat said enthusiastically. "He had an inside man in the department. Maybe we can get to Ontiveros through this person."

"I'll call Gleason. Hopefully he knows the forensic tech's name by now, and with Gina in danger, I think he'll tell me." Derrick dug out his phone and thumbed through his address book. He tossed up a prayer that the detective would have a change of heart. The moment Gleason answered, Derrick launched into his story. "Do you have the name of Ontiveros's guy in the forensics department?"

Gleason sighed. "You know I can't tell you that."

"Things have changed. Gina's in danger. If Ontiveros has her, we need to find him, and your guy is the only way I can do it." Derrick could hear the desperation in his own voice and forced himself to calm down before he scared Gleason away. "Please. I'm begging you. Tell me who it is."

Gleason sighed again, then said, "We're looking at Bo McClain, but I don't really like him for this. I'm thinking someone is trying to pin it on him."

Derrick cupped his hand over the phone and looked at Dani. "Find everything you can on a Bo McClain. Works in the SPD forensics division."

"He's a well-respected cop," Gleason continued. "Twenty years on the street before the stress of the job got to him. Decided to get the necessary education and moved to forensics, where he's been a valuable member of the team for the past five years. Doesn't sound like a guy who's on the take to me."

"Where can I find him?"

"Sorry, man. I shouldn't have given you his name—telling you where he lives would be going too far. I'll be glad to get an alert out on Gina and work the scene for you, but that's all I can do."

"The FBI's already on scene."

"The Bureau?"

"We've been using an agent's home as our safe house. She was attacked during the abduction."

"I still want to process the scene. Give me the address and a description of Gina, so I can issue the alert."

Derrick provided Tracy's address and described Gina, the process bringing her vividly to his mind, making him think of all he might lose if anything happened to her.

"I'll get this to dispatch," Gleason said. "But it would help if you had a picture of her."

"No picture," Derrick said.

"Okay, we'll look for a driver's license photo then. I'll call if the alert produces any results."

He disconnected, but despite Gleason's help, Derrick's worry escalated to a frenzy. He cared about Gina. Deeply. And he'd do anything to have a future with her and Sophia.

He relayed his conversation with Gleason then turned to Dani, who had her laptop open. "Anything?"

She swiveled the computer. "I've got McClain's address. He's less than ten minutes from here."

"Then let's get over there and see if he can lead us to Ontiveros." Derrick didn't wait for his sisters to agree but charged for the door. He took the steps two at a time, and by the time Dani climbed into the passenger seat and Kat slid in the back, he had the engine running.

"I'll put his address in the GPS." Dani punched it in.

"Kat, call Tracy," Derrick said as he merged onto the road. "She might have located something to help."

Dani opened her computer. "I'll keep looking into McClain as we drive."

The screen of Dani's laptop cast a white light over her face while Kat talked with Tracy. The conversation ended almost as quickly as it started.

"Tracy hasn't located any leads," Kat said.

Frustrated, Derrick pressed harder on the gas pedal and careened in and out of traffic.

"Slow it down, bro," Dani said without looking up. "It won't help Gina if we don't make it there."

Derrick lifted his foot a smidge but kept the car moving above the speed limit.

Kat leaned over the seat. "We won't get there if an officer pulls us over, either."

Knowing both his sisters spoke the truth, Derrick eased off the gas and slowed to a moderate speed, but his insides continued to race with fear. He couldn't lose Gina. Not now. Not after he'd found her again. Especially not when it was his fault that she'd been taken. His sisters had said not to blame himself, but how could he not?

"Bingo! I'm in McClain's bank account." Dani ran her finger down the screen. "This is promising—he's deposited several large sums of cash recently."

"Then it's looking good for him to lead us to Ontiveros," Kat said.

Derrick felt a moment of relief. "Cross-reference the deposit dates to the cases thrown out for ballistics issues."

From the corner of his eye, he saw the computer flash again.

"All of them jibe," Dani soon confirmed.

"Good work, Dani," Kat said as her phone rang. "It's Mitch." She leaned back and answered with a tone she reserved just for her husband.

The GPS announced their destination on the right, and Derrick pulled into the parking lot in front of a high-rise apartment building. As he hunted for a parking space, he heard Kat bring Mitch up to speed on McClain. She suddenly stopped talking, and the quiet ratcheted up Derrick's concern.

"Hold on," she said. "I'll put you on speaker so you can tell Derrick and Dani."

"Go ahead, Mitch." Derrick slid the car into a space.

"We located the boat we believe Lilly was killed on. We've lifted several good latents. My guys are running the prints right now."

"Perfect timing," Dani called out. "McClain is former Army, so start with military databases."

"Army?" Derrick shot Dani a look. "You think he acted as the sniper the other day, not Ontiveros or one of his men?"

"Could be," Dani said. "He was a Ranger."

The Army's equivalent to a Navy SEAL. Meaning he was dangerous and deadly. If he was the one targeting Gina, they'd simply gotten lucky that he hadn't succeeded in killing her yet. Rescuing her had just moved into an arena that would challenge all of their resources.

After a few minutes of casing the building, the siblings decided on a surprise attack and slipped up the stairs to McClain's apartment. Dani picked the lock and silently swung the door open. Darkness greeted them.

Derrick let his eyes adjust to the blackness lit only with small LED lights from electronic equipment. Once he was able to see, he signaled his sisters to move in, and they crept into the apartment.

Room by room they stealthily searched. Room by room they came up empty and moved on. At the last room, Derrick's heart sank.

"She's not here." Derrick holstered his weapon and forced away his disappointment. He couldn't let this setback keep him from working smart. "There's bound to be a lead here. We just need to find it."

Together, they moved back to the living room, where he flipped on the overhead light.

"I'll take the computer." Dani headed for a laptop on the coffee table.

"Desk," Derrick called out and went straight to a mass of papers piled high.

"With the mess on that desk, you can use my help." Kat joined him, lifted a stack of papers and quickly sifted through them.

Derrick bent over another pile and caught a glimpse of a photo peeking from under unpaid bills. He jerked out the picture of a burly man standing on board a speedboat identical to Quentin's boat.

He held the photo out for Kat. "Boat's the same make and model as Quentin's. If this is McClain's boat, he could've been the one who fired on us at the marina."

Kat looked at Dani. "Can you pull up McClain's driver's license so we can compare it with this picture?"

"Sure thing." Dani clicked away while Derrick and Kat joined her. She held up the computer, displaying McClain's ID.

"It's him all right," Kat said. "It's looking more and more like McClain's the one who's been trying to kill Gina all along and he's got her now."

Derrick shook his head. "I don't like the thought that we're searching for an Army Ranger. Means he could be ruthless. Gina might already be dead."

"Or not," Dani said.

Derrick cast her a questioning look.

"Think about it," she said. "He's been trying to kill Gina for days, and suddenly when he has the perfect opportunity to kill her, he doesn't take it. Why not?"

"Maybe he's supposed to turn her over to Ontiveros," Derrick suggested.

"Or as a forensic expert, he doesn't want to leave any incriminating evidence behind," Kat offered. "So perhaps he plans to kill her in his boat and dump the body in the water, same as Lilly."

Dani nodded. "I always wondered why the killer took Lilly out to the river. This would explain it."

The thought of Gina in a boat with a gun to her head made Derrick wince, but he refused to dwell on it. "Then we need to figure out where he moors his boat."

"There's got to be information about his slip rental in that mess on his desk." Kat hurried back to the desk.

The three of them rifled through the paperwork.

"Here." Dani held up a bill.

Derrick snatched it from her hand. "It's the same marina Quentin uses. It's only a few miles from here. Maybe we can catch McClain."

Dani's forehead furrowed. "He's got a good head start on us and could've already put out to sea."

"Then we need a boat, too," Derrick said. "Let's head over to the marina, and we can figure out how to get one on the way."

They wasted no time rushing down the stairs and were soon on the road again winding through traffic.

"We should call Gleason," Kat suggested from the backseat. "Since we now have more information on McClain's potential involvement, Gleason might agree to help find Gina."

"It couldn't hurt." Derrick handed his phone to Dani so he could concentrate on driving. "His name's in my contact list. Put him on speaker."

When Gleason answered, Derrick quickly updated him on McClain's military ties, his finances and the boat. "This is the probable cause you need to haul McClain in for questioning."

"Man," Gleason replied. "I'd never have imagined I was wrong about him. He seemed like such a standup guy."

"You work as a detective long enough and you learn not to let anything surprise you."

"I suppose you're right."

"So are you going to help us?" Derrick pushed again.

"I'd like to." He paused, as if trying to decide what to do. "But you got the information without a warrant, so it's of no use to me. The best I can do is work on legally obtaining the same info."

"Gina needs your help now, not after you repeat the work we've already done," Derrick yelled at him. "Color outside the box for once and bring this guy in."

"You may have operated outside the law when you were on the force, but that's not how we do things in California."

Derrick ground his teeth. "At least put a bulletin out on him."

"No," Gleason said firmly. "It would do more harm than good. McClain still has buddies on the force who'd see the alert and warn him. If he thinks we're coming for him, he might do something rash."

"He's already done something rash," Derrick

shouted. "He's kidnapped a woman." *The woman I love.*

"But she could still be alive, and I won't go off half-cocked and make the situation worse."

"Fine," Derrick shouted. "But be advised if anything happens to Gina, I'll hold you personally responsible." Fuming, Derrick slammed a hand against the wheel.

"You want me to hang up?" Dani asked.

Derrick nodded. "I've never felt so helpless in my life," he said. But even as he spoke the words, the memory of his parents' deaths flashed into his mind, and he knew today's feeling wasn't new to him.

He couldn't believe how fresh the grief felt. And the guilt. Both emotions were still there. Holding him captive. That's why he'd let Gina walk out of his life. Just as she'd said—he didn't feel like he deserved to be happy.

*Help me find her, Father. Please help me find her.*

Dani set his phone in the console. "I'll try to locate McClain's boat information. If he has a GPS system installed, I might be able to pinpoint his location."

"Good. Do that."

Kat leaned forward. "And why don't we call Quentin? He might be able to get the Coast Guard to send someone after Gina."

"Better yet, we could use his boat to go after her ourselves." He flashed a look at Dani, who was already at work on her computer. "Quentin's number's in my cell, Kat. Call him and put it on speaker."

Quentin answered on the third ring, and Derrick raced ahead with his story. "Can you get the Coast Guard to dispatch a boat for her?"

"I'll call them, but it'll be faster if I go after her myself."

"Not without me."

Quentin didn't respond.

"C'mon, man," Derrick said. "After the way you stonewalled us, you owe me that much—not to mention what you owe Gina."

"Agreed. I'll meet you at the marina."

"McClain's boat is the same make and model as yours. We'll text his photo to you in case you arrive before us and he's still at the pier."

Derrick could hear Quentin was already on the move, and he grunted his acknowledgment.

"Hang up the phone, Kat," Derrick said. "We have a rescue to perform."

# NINETEEN

As they turned onto the drive leading to the marina, Gina frantically searched for a way to escape her captor. She could think of only one reason he was taking her to a boat. Just as with Lilly, he planned to kill her and dump her body where no one would ever find her. She needed to get away, but she had little hope of escape with her wrist securely cuffed to the door. Maybe if she got him to tell her his plan, she'd be better prepared to make a run for it when he unlocked the cuff. She'd have to ease into it.

She looked at him, searching for an idea of what to say. "You don't look like a drug dealer."

He laughed. "What do I look like then?"

"A law-abiding citizen."

He glanced at her. "Better than that, I'm a former cop."

Her heart dropped. If he admitted this, it meant he planned to kill her. Even more reason to keep asking questions.

"I wondered about the handcuffs," she said lightly,

hoping to play down her worry. "How does a former cop get mixed up with Ontiveros?"

"Not that it's any of your business, but I got tired of pulling lowlifes off the street day after day only for them to have some lawyer get their charges thrown out. Then they'd reoffend, and I'd just have to haul them in again. I started drinking to blow off the pressure. Before long, the drinking carried over to my work. My partner was gonna report me, so I came up with the bright idea to move to forensics. Was a good gig until I fell off the wagon and ran up some gambling debts."

"And let me guess, that's where Ontiveros came in," Gina said.

"Yep. He was facing a murder rap. He needed someone to falsify ballistics to get him off. I needed the cash for my debts. Voila. A partnership was formed."

"The murder was Perry Axton's, right?"

He glanced at her. "I see that pretty boy you hired did his homework."

His comment reminded her of the family's joke about how pretty Derrick was. The longing to have him by her side nearly brought her to tears. She clenched her teeth until the feeling passed and looked at her abductor again. "What I don't get is how you went from changing a report to trying to kill me."

"Simple. You saw the log that could put Ontiveros away for life and me for a good long time. You couldn't live to tell about it."

She shook her head. "But murder? Why not just go to jail for tampering with evidence? You'd get out a lot sooner than if you were caught and convicted of murder."

"That's true, *if* Ontiveros let me live to see that day. But I'm here to tell you, sister, that he wouldn't have let me get to trial. I needed to clean up this mess or start digging my own grave."

"So you killed Jon," she said with sad resignation.

"I didn't kill him," he spit out forcefully. "Ontiveros did. I'm former military. Your brother didn't deserve to die like the other lowlifes Ontiveros offed."

"Then why are you still working for him?"

He sneered. "You don't walk away from someone like him. At least not alive."

"And that means you have to kill for him?"

He shrugged as if life meant nothing to him and pointed his car toward the dock.

The choppy water let her know what she was in for, and her pulse ratcheted higher. "And now you're going to kill me like you killed Lilly, right?"

"If she'd listened to me, she wouldn't have had to die," he said as he parked near a boat identical to Quentin's. "I thought she was you at first and tried to restrain her, but she pulled off my mask. She could ID me, so she had to go."

"I suppose you shot her on the river to ensure no one would ever find her."

"Nah, I'm a forensic tech, remember? I took her out there to get rid of any trace evidence." He shifted into Park and came around the car to open the door. He pointed his gun at her chest and gave her the key to remove the cuff from the door. "Step out nice and slow with your hands in front."

When she did, he grabbed the dangling cuff and dragged her onto the boat.

"Sit." He shoved her down and waved his gun at her. "I'm going to untie the boat. Don't try anything stupid."

She looked around for a way out. He hadn't cuffed her to the boat, so maybe she could jump overboard. No. The water was too shallow to hide her, and he'd simply use his gun to end her life before she could take cover. She searched again, hoping someone would stroll down the pier, but the only movement this late at night was the water lapping against the boats. She'd have to wait for a better time.

What better time? Once out in the ocean, she wouldn't escape alive. Maybe she could distract him and delay their departure so help could arrive.

She offered a quick prayer then looked at her abductor. "You never told me your name."

He didn't look up from his task. "No need for you to know."

She tried another topic. "So you brought me out here to get rid of evidence, like you did with Lilly. I wouldn't have thought you'd risk me escaping."

His ice-cold eyes raked over her. "I'd think twice about taking off, if I was you." He aimed his gun at her.

Visions of him pointing a gun at her in her apartment came flooding back. She couldn't count on this one jamming. She'd have to play down her escape.

"I'm not trying to escape," she lied as convincingly as she could. "I simply wondered after all those attempts to kill me, why you haven't taken the chance now that you finally have it."

"Right now you're worth more to me alive than dead." He moved to the other tie-down.

"I don't understand," Gina said.

"Your little team of investigators ratted me out to the cops." He snarled. "Fortunately I got wind of it in time, but they'll soon be looking for me. You're my ticket out of town."

"A hostage?" Gina said hopefully. "Does that mean you don't plan to kill me?"

"That's a good question." He tossed the rope into the boat and picked up his gun. "One I'm sure you don't want to hear the answer to."

As Derrick swung the car into the marina's parking lot, Kat's phone rang. "It's Mitch again."

Derrick piloted the car toward Quentin's boat while he put Mitch on speaker.

"I've got an ID for the fingerprints," he said.

"Let me guess," Kat replied. "It's a former Army Ranger named Bo McClain."

"You knew?"

"We weren't positive, but you just confirmed it."

"Any word on Gina?"

Kat brought him up to speed then quickly said goodbye while Derrick parked as close to Quentin's boat as possible.

"I'm outta here." Derrick jumped out and checked his ammo. Kat and Dani did the same.

"No one's coming with me," Derrick said.

Kat furrowed her brow. "Not a good idea."

"Someone needs to stay here in case the police or Coast Guard actually dispatches help."

"I can do that while I keep looking for McClain's GPS device," Dani said.

Kat crossed her arms in a stubborn stance. "That frees me up to come with you."

"It'll be dangerous out there, and I can't be thinking about your safety. The rescue will take my full focus and having you there will distract me."

"Gee, if only I was trained for situations like this and knew how to handle myself." Kat frowned at him.

He shook his head and grabbed extra ammo.

"Fine." Kat sighed. "I don't want to make the situation worse. If you think my going with you would do that, then I'll stay here."

"Thanks, Kat." He gave her a quick hug. "If I can get a phone signal out there, I'll call you as soon as we find her."

"Bring her back safely," Dani said, but Derrick was already running for the boat and didn't respond.

By the time he got there, Quentin was untying the mooring ropes. "I saw a guy matching McClain's description taking off when I arrived."

"And Gina?" Derrick asked.

"Didn't see her."

"So this could be someone else."

"Could be, but there's little traffic out here at night, so our best bet is to head out in the direction of that boat and hope it was McClain."

"Is the Guard on the way?"

"Not yet." He tossed his rope into the boat. "If we get close enough to McClain to prove he has Gina, I'll radio in our coordinates and they've promised to respond."

"That's better than nothing I guess." Derrick followed Quentin onboard.

Quentin went straight for the steering wheel. "This is going to be fast and rough." He glanced at Derrick. "If you can't handle it, you'd best bail now."

Derrick jerked his head at the open waters. "Just go."

"Okay then," Quentin said doubtfully. "Have a seat."

He fired up the powerful motor and eased away from the pier. Once they hit open water, he accelerated hard, pushing Derrick's back against the seat and reminding him of a carnival ride. The front section of the boat lifted in the air, and they flew over choppy waves spitting seawater in their faces.

Derrick rose to his knees to scan the horizon. Even with a full moon, he couldn't see far ahead. Quentin kept them moving at a steady clip, but suddenly he throttled down and killed the lights. He lifted what had to be night-vision binoculars. "There's a boat ahead on the starboard side. A man is at the helm— about the right size and shape to be McClain. I see another person on board in the back. Smaller. Seated. Could be Gina."

He passed the binoculars to Derrick, who confirmed Quentin's take. "You're the expert out here. How do we approach?"

"He's not moving as fast as we were, so we should be able to catch him after we power back up. Though once he sees our lights he's likely to take off."

"Can we run in the dark?"

"Not at the speeds we'll be traveling." Quentin tapped the binoculars. "Keep the boat in sight and warn me if he changes course."

"Do you really think we have a chance?"

Quentin shrugged. "We'll just have to hope McClain is too busy to see us coming."


Gina tried to sweep the hair out of her face, but it made no difference. Despite her efforts, strands caught the wind and bit into her cheek. Chilled and wet, she huddled forward to avoid the stinging spray.

The farther they traveled from shore, the more she feared no one would ever find her. If they didn't, who would look after Sophia? Jon had died so recently that she hadn't arranged for Sophia's care in the event of her death. Her sweet little Sophia, all alone. Gina could hardly bear the thought.

*No,* she warned herself. *Don't think that way. Only a quitter has those thoughts, and you are not a quitter.*

Maybe Derrick had located her and was on his way.

*Derrick.* The man she'd worked so hard not to fall for these past few days. But it didn't matter how hard she struggled, the feelings were there. And real. Thinking about losing her life made the thought of him not committing irrelevant. He wanted to change, and she wanted to help him. She knew he'd never deliberately hurt her or Sophia, so she'd trust him and take the risk.

Her captor suddenly downshifted the boat, the massive bow setting into the water. She sat up and watched for a chance to free herself. He punched a few buttons on a device that looked like a portable GPS system then slammed his fist against the boat and spit out a long string of curse words.

"Something wrong?" she asked, hoping the question didn't make him angrier.

"Nothing I can't fix." He dug into a storage compartment and came out holding a flashlight. He shone it on the navigation system and started pressing buttons.

With his focus on the problem, Gina decided it would be the perfect time to act. If she caught him from behind with a full-body check, she might be able to launch him into the water. But it would only work if she hit him hard in the upper body, gaining enough momentum to clear the side.

Praying for help, she slowly got to her feet and inched forward. His head remained bent over his task. She continued to assess her plan as she moved. She couldn't ease up beside him or he'd see her. One sudden lunge was her only chance. She readied herself, curling forward for maximum oomph. Hoping her frozen muscles would cooperate, she set her feet in position to lunge—but the hum of an engine coming from the ocean behind them made her captor suddenly spin and see her.

He smacked her down, causing her head to slam against the hard molded plastic of a seat. Warm, sticky blood dripped into her eye. She pressed a hand against the wound to stop the bleeding. Pain shot through her skull at the pressure, but she kept pushing, until the intensity made her woozy.

She pulled her hand away and tried to get to her feet.

He pressed a booted foot on her side as he scanned the ocean behind them. "If you know what's good for you, you'll stay down."

The hum of a large motor grew closer.

*Please, God, let it be Derrick. Or the Coast Guard. Someone, anyone to end this nightmare.*

Her captor dug in a storage bench next to her and extracted a rifle. He kept his foot on her side as he loaded cartridges into the gun.

*Keep whoever's in the approaching boat safe.*

Her captor removed his foot and pressed the rifle's barrel against the side of her head. She cringed, but he pressed harder. "This is how easily I can end your life if you move even a fraction of an inch from your spot. Got that?"

"Yes," she said, her voice trembling and revealing her inner turmoil.

He lifted his foot and slowly backed to the driver's seat, the rifle butt lodged against his chest. At the wheel, he rested the gun at his side then rammed the speed control forward. He grabbed an elastic strap and secured the steering wheel to maintain the course bearing.

Moving unsteadily, he passed her and planted his knees on the backseat with his upper body lying prone on the rear of the boat. He hefted his rifle into firing position and waited.

As they rode the choppy waters, the other boat's motor roared closer. She feared the minute he confirmed the boat was here to rescue her he'd open fire. She couldn't let her captor shoot anyone in that boat. Or her, for that matter.

She looked around and spotted a life jacket tucked under the seat. If he started firing, she could lunge at him to knock him off course. Even if she plunged into the water with him, the vest would keep her afloat.

She slowly shrugged into the vest and offered a prayer. If she failed now, not only might she die at this crazed man's hands, but if Derrick was in the boat behind them, he could lose his life, as well.

# TWENTY

As they moved in sight of McClain's boat, Quentin slowed.

"What're you doing, man?" Derrick reached for the throttle. "They'll get away."

Quentin blocked his hand. "Trust me. I've done this many times and I know what I'm doing."

"But he has Gina. I saw her in the binoculars. We have to get moving—now!"

Quentin ignored his plea and moved to a storage box where he pulled out two rifles, both with night vision scopes. He handed one to Derrick along with a box of cartridges. "These are copper sabot slugs designed to pierce the boat and kill the engine."

"You can do that?" Derrick asked, hope coming to life.

"Oh, yeah." Quentin grinned.

"What if an aggressive action like that makes McClain hurt Gina?"

"He won't." Quentin finished loading his rifle and snapped it closed. "Once his boat is disabled, he'l have no way out other than through us. She's his only bargaining chip."

"But then we have to talk him into surrendering."

Quentin grabbed his boat radio and held it up. "That's where the Coast Guard comes in. If he doesn't surrender to them, you or I can take him out. That is, if you're a good enough shot."

"I can take him, so let's do this," Derrick said and added a prayer for help.

Quentin radioed in their location and Derrick tried to call Kat and Dani, but he had no signal. He heard the operator promise to dispatch a boat, and he forced himself to believe this would work.

Quentin picked up his rifle. "You take over the controls and get us as close as you can. If McClain starts firing on us, use the rifle to return fire. Got it?"

Derrick nodded.

"What are you waiting for?" Quentin asked. "We've got a damsel in distress to rescue."

Derrick rested the rifle next to his leg then throttled the boat into high speed. They flew over the water and slowly gained on the other boat.

"That's close enough," Quentin shouted. "Now hold her steady." Quentin planted his arms and sighted his rifle. He cracked off a shot, and Derrick heard the other motor cut out.

Grinning, Quentin looked back. "We better hope it's McClain's boat or we'll have an expensive engine to repair."

Suddenly a rifle retort fractured the quiet, and

Derrick lifted the binoculars. The shooter lurched to a standing position, and Gina flew into him, sending both of them overboard.

"No!" Derrick dropped the binoculars. "Gina's in the water. I'm going in after her."

"I'll go, I'm trained for this kind of rescue," Quentin argued.

Derrick ignored him, shed his jacket and grabbed a life preserver.

"Fine, but wait until I bring us closer." Quentin grabbed the throttle and shot the boat forward.

When they neared the other craft and Quentin slowed, Derrick plunged into the icy water. Keeping his eyes out for McClain, Derrick stroked his way toward the spot where he saw Gina go in.

"Gina!" Derrick screamed. "Call out."

"Here," she said, her voice weaker than Derrick would like to hear.

He pummeled the water with his hands and kicked his legs though his muscles screamed in protest. Nearing the boat, he couldn't see Gina anywhere nor did he see McClain.

"Where are you, sweetheart?" he called again.

"Here." Her voice came from the back side of the boat.

He swam to her. The cold should have slowed him, but a burst of adrenaline fueled his body.

Derrick heard a splash and soon Quentin shouted. "McClain's out cold. Must've hit his head on the boat. I have him."

Great. Now Derrick didn't have to worry about that threat. He used the edge of McClain's boat to pull himself around the corner. Gina clung to a landing pad on the back.

"Thank You, God," Derrick shouted and pulled her into his arms.

"You f-f-found me-e-e," she said, her words broken by chattering teeth.

"Of course, I did." He wanted to press the hair from her face and kiss her until they were both breathless, but getting her out of the water was his top priority. He lifted her onto the landing pad and pulled himself up. Love for this amazing, strong woman filled his heart. Now she just had to survive the frigid cold so he could shower her with those kisses and tell her.

The Coast Guardsman poked his head through the cabin door. "We'll have you on shore in no time, ma'am."

"Thank you." Gina sighed at the warmth of the cabin, where she sat all alone. The Coast Guard had arrived shortly after Derrick hoisted her into McClain's boat. She'd wanted to stay with him, but he and Quentin were dealing with her kidnapper's arrest.

Bo McClain, Derrick had told her, was the man who'd held her captive for a terrifying ride. The man hadn't killed her brother, but had made it possible for Ontiveros to escape prosecution for killing him, and would be charged with Lilly's murder as soon as the district attorney could draw up the papers.

Derrick stepped inside the small room, his presence filling the space. "Quentin's staying with McClain until he's turned over to local authorities."

"I still can't believe you figured out what he was up to and then actually found us."

"I have to admit it was a challenge, but I wasn't going to give up until we had you home safe and sound."

She took his chilly hand. "I owe your whole family more than I can ever repay."

He shrugged. "What can I say? It's just what we do."

"And what you do is amazing." She squeezed his hand. "You've become a man I could never have imagined when we were together."

"I can say the same thing about you." He tucked a soggy strand of hair behind her ear, sending shivers down her back.

"So I've become quite a man then?" she joked to deflect from the love burning in her heart that she hoped he returned.

"Trust me." He gazed into her eyes. "There's nothing manly about you." He slid his fingers into her hair and cupped the back of her head. "Nothing at all."

As he lowered his head, his lips inches from hers, she heard a male clear his throat near the door and pulled back.

"I hate to interrupt," the same guardsman said from the doorway, this time with a grin on his face. "We're preparing to dock, and I thought you'd want to get out of here and into some dry clothes as soon as possible."

"That we do." Derrick stood and helped Gina to her feet. His gaze lingered on her face then, with a long exhale, he turned and stepped onto the deck.

Her heart and mind a mass of confusion, she trailed behind him as they pulled into the Coast Guard station to find Kat and Dani standing on the dock.

Though Gina was grateful to them for all their help, she wished they weren't there. She wanted to ride back to the house alone with Derrick so she could tell him that she wanted him in her and Sophia's life. Now she'd have to wait until they were alone and she only hoped with the passing of time she didn't lose the courage to be honest with him.

In a funk, Derrick paced the deck at Tracy's house. Normally he'd stop to enjoy the wooded ravine. To let the peace and tranquility calm his angst—but there was no calm for him now. He was hopelessly and totally in love with Gina. He wanted to tell her, but fear clung to him like a spider web, tangling him in confusion.

God had made it clear that his life had mirrored Gina's, and instead of dealing with the loss of his parents, he'd let his guilt and insecurities control him. Gina had let her father's actions control her, too. They differed only in that she'd searched for someone who would put her first in his life while he'd put up a wall to avoid all serious relationships.

She walked past the window, cradling Sophia in her arms, reminding him of how successful she'd been in moving on. He wanted the same thing. He also wanted her and Sophia in his life so badly, he ached and yet, he was too afraid to do something about it.

Kat stepped outside. "Mind if I join you?"

He shrugged, knowing she was coming out here to lecture him for being so standoffish with Gina.

She marched right up to him. "Remember when Dani and Luke were clearly smitten but avoiding each other?"

The memory of the two of them refusing to acknowledge their feelings last year came back to him as he nodded.

"Do you remember what I told you?"

"Not really."

"I promised that when you had someone perfect in your life that you were avoiding, I'd tell you to let go of whatever excuse you were using not to get involved."

"Oh, that," he said and turned toward the ravine.

She grabbed his arm and jerked him around. "That time has come, and if you don't get over whatever is keeping you from Gina, she's going to walk out of your life again. Permanently. And that adorable little girl is going with her."

He glanced inside the family room, and a longing to be with her sent a raw ache into his gut. But he couldn't move.

"Remember what Dad always said when you hung back at new adventures?" Kat asked, her tone softer now.

"It's time to fish or cut the bait."

"Yeah, it's that time now. Enough of your indecisiveness. It'll only lead to a lonely life filled with anxiety."

"I know, but…"

"Trust that God has brought Gina back into your life for a reason." Kat rested a hand on his shoulder. "Don't let her go. Tell her how you feel, and let God work on whatever's bothering you."

"You make it sound so simple."

"Simple?" She laughed. "No, but well worth it. I oughta know. Life with Mitch is so much richer than it ever was without him, and I almost threw that away just like you're doing. Learn from my mistake."

He studied his sister for a moment and thought of all of his siblings and their lives filled with joy. He wanted that. She was right. He had to go for it, and no matter the outcome, let God work it for their good.

"Thanks, Kit Kat," he said, hugging her hard. "Now make yourself scarce. I have to tell a woman I love her."

Kat giggled like a child on Christmas. "My work here is done. With all of us in a committed relationship, I lay down my job as the family matchmaker."

"Thank goodness." He dramatically wiped a hand across his brow. "I don't think we could've survived any more of it."

Laughing together, they entered the house. Gina was heading for the bedroom with a sleeping Sophia on her shoulder.

"Wait, Gina," Derrick called out. "Can I talk to you before you put her down for the night?"

She faced him, a big question in her eyes.

"I'll keep everyone out of your hair." Kat stopped to squeeze Gina's hand then hurried out of the room.

Derrick joined Gina. "There's something I need to tell you."

"Okay," she said hesitantly.

"You must know by now that I still have feelings for you."

She smiled shyly. "I hoped you did."

He pressed his hand over hers where it rested on Sophia's back. "For this little one, too." He shook his head. "Surprised me, but she took over my heart when I wasn't looking." He lifted his hand to cup the side of Gina's face. "A heart you've always had."

She leaned into his hand. "You've always had mine, too."

"I love you, Gina, and if you'll give me a second chance, I'll work night and day to prove I'm here for the long haul. For you *and* Bug."

"I love you, too." She moved closer to him, her eyes brimming with tears. "And I don't care if you can't make a firm commitment right now. My time with McClain made me see life is too short to let worries stop me from enjoying life. We'll just take things one day at a time."

Derrick kissed Sophia's soft curls. "Then maybe we should put Bug down for the night so we can start to work on that."

"What did you have in mind?" Gina asked in a breathless whisper.

He leaned forward and settled his lips on hers, kissing her the way he'd wanted to the first night they'd reconnected.

After a long kiss, she pulled back. "Hmm. We most definitely need to put Sophia down for the night and get started on our life together."

# EPILOGUE

Derrick brushed his hand down the sleeve of his new suit and looked in the mirror in the church dressing room. The men in his wedding party were standing around talking sports and looking about as uncomfortable in their formal attire as Derrick felt. The group included Ethan, Cole, Mitch and Luke. They all wore black suits chosen by Gina with crisp white shirts and muted ties. She'd selected a tie for Derrick with hints of red to go with the wedding colors.

Derrick took a deep breath and exhaled out his prewedding jitters. He'd never been more certain of anything than marrying Gina, but the waiting was making him crazy. He slipped his finger behind his tie to loosen the knot.

"Don't tell me." Cole came up behind him and clamped his hand on a shoulder. "You're rethinking this decision and you're gonna choke."

Derrick shook his head. "I'm not used to wearing a tie anymore, and I tied it too tight is all."

Cole met Derrick's gaze in the mirror. "If you feel like running, it's nothing to be ashamed off."

"Stop it, Cole." Ethan joined them. "We've been waiting a long time to get this one hitched, and you're not helping."

Derrick turned and looked at his wedding party. "You can all relax. I'm not running."

"That's good," Mitch said. "Kat would have my hide if I let you out of my sight."

"She tasked you with watching me?" Derrick asked.

"Yeah, but don't tell her I mentioned it."

"Dani gave me similar instructions," Luke admitted with a wry smile.

Derrick shook his head and looked at Ethan and Cole. "You two get the same thing from Alyssa and Jennie?"

"Not me," Ethan said. "But then Jennie's too busy trailing after a toddler these days to notice much else."

"Alyssa's had her hands full getting the twins ready to be in the wedding party." Cole frowned. "Who knew it took so much work to be a flower girl and ring bearer?"

"Like I said, you can all relax," Derrick said. "I get that my past makes you think I might want to bail, but I'm not going anywhere except to the front of the church."

An alarm dinged on Ethan's watch, and he grinned

at Derrick. "Nice to be the one in charge of time around you, man."

Derrick had gladly given up his time obsession and relaxed in a way he never had. But today was no time to relax. He was getting married. At the thought of seeing Gina in her dress and finally calling her his wife, his heart turned over.

"Let's do this." He tugged his jacket, looked at his reflection in the mirror one final time and went to meet his bride.

He couldn't choose between his brothers for the best-man role, so he opted not to choose at all. All of the men would stand in front with him as the bridesmaids and Gina walked down the aisle. That meant he'd have to hold on to the rings himself, but he liked the feel of them in his pocket, as if they somehow guaranteed that Gina would be his.

She'd followed his lead and hadn't selected a maid of honor either, but embraced Derrick's sisters and sisters-in-law equally. Gina's father would preside over the service, but first he'd walk her down the aisle.

As the men took their places near the altar, Bobby slipped away from Mitch's sister, Angie, and bolted toward Ethan. "Daddy!"

Ethan picked him up and gave Derrick an apologetic look. "Sorry, man. He may have refused to walk down the aisle today, but looks like he wants to be in the wedding after all."

"No problem." Derrick smiled at his brother. "He's just proving he has the Justice stubbornness."

"As if that was ever in question."

Derrick laughed and ran his gaze over the sanctuary filled with friends and family. He caught familiar faces and smiled. He was here to declare his love for Gina before God and his loved ones, and the moment couldn't be more perfect for him.

The preservice music stopped and the string quartet played a familiar song that Gina had often performed on her violin in college as her mother and grandmother came down the aisle and sat in the front pew.

As Jennie rounded the corner wearing a black bridesmaid gown and started down the aisle, Derrick cast a glance at Ethan, who beamed with happiness. Bobby squirmed from Ethan's arms and ran to Jennie, who took his hand and continued to the front of the church as if Bobby's impromptu role had been planned.

Wearing a similar gown, Dani entered the sanctuary, and Luke drew in a deep breath before a broad smile took over. Next came Kat, her belly swollen with her first child. Her eyes immediately went to Mitch's. Usually a tough guy, his expression softened at the sight of her. Alyssa entered last so the twins, Brianna and Riley, could follow her down the aisle.

"Breathtaking," Cole whispered, then smiled.

Brianna and Riley trailed behind, Sophia's hands firmly clasped in theirs. She'd mastered walking two months ago, and Derrick hoped she'd handle the event well.

Shy, Brianna's steps faltered, but Riley said something that urged her forward.

"You can do it, Bri," Cole whispered, giving his recently adopted daughter the encouragement she needed to keep going.

Derrick hoped when the day came to have children with Gina that his kids would be as supportive of each other as Riley and Brianna were. As the trio reached the front pew, Sophia caught sight of Derrick and broke free.

She toddled toward him and said, "Up."

Derrick scooped her into his arms. "Hi, Bug."

She planted her chubby hands on his cheeks and rubbed his nose with hers as she'd come to do in the past month. He heard sighs from the guests, and he knew this would be a memory he'd cherish forever.

The music changed into a fanfare, and a thrill of anticipation ran over him. "It's time, Bug." He turned her so she could see Gina walk down the aisle.

Derrick watched over Sophia's bouncy curls as his bride rounded the corner. Derrick took in her strapless gown with a million sparkling beads on the bodice and skirt. She'd chosen not to wear a veil, and her hair was pulled up, accentuating her long neck and regal posture.

Her gaze met his, and he didn't care if anyone else remained in the room. He was marrying the woman of his dreams while holding the precious child who would soon be his daughter, and he was the happiest man on the planet.

As Val adjusted Gina's train, she scanned the front of the church. The women looked radiant in their gowns while Brianna and Riley looked adorable.

Wait. Where was Sophia? She had to be there.

Gina's focus slid over the handsome men, then zeroed in on Derrick. A sigh of contentment slipped out when she saw him holding Sophia. The dark suit highlighted his blond hair and the white shirt brought out his skin bronzed by the summer sun, but when she met his gaze, she couldn't look away.

For years, she'd wondered what it would've been like if they hadn't broken up. Never had she imagined her heart would swell with such happiness.

"Your flowers." Val handed Gina her bouquet with dark red and white roses.

"Thank you for all of your help."

"Jon would've loved this day." Tears filled Val's eyes. "I'm sure he's with us in spirit."

"I agree." Gina gave Val a hug. "Now go join Quentin and your kids."

Gina released Val before she started crying, too.

"Ready?" her father asked as he smiled at her.

Thrilled that he was finally present for an important event in her life, she nodded and slipped her arm into his. The quartet began playing the traditional wedding march, and Gina headed down the aisle. She wanted to look around, to take in all of the people who'd come to wish them well, but she couldn't pull her eyes from Sophia and Derrick.

Anticipation for when they'd officially become a family sent goose bumps down her arms. After much deliberation and consultation with professionals, they'd decided to raise Sophia as their own child. When she was old enough to understand, they'd tell her about her birth parents and make sure she knew how much they'd loved her, but for now, she was fully Gina and Derrick's daughter.

When they reached the front, her father escorted her up the stairs.

"Mama," Sophia called out and reached for Gina.

Gina passed her flowers to Jennie and took Sophia as Derrick moved into place next to them. He circled his arm around her back and pulled her closer. Her father began, and despite Sophia's occasional squirmy behavior, the ceremony went off without a hitch.

"May I present," her father announced as Derrick and Gina turned to face their guests, "Mr. and Mrs. Derrick Justice and Sophia, their precious child I'm proud to call my granddaughter."

The guests erupted in applause and Sophia clapped with them, sending broad smiles across the room.

"Ready for our first act as a married couple?" Derrick asked.

"Ready."

Derrick took Sophia and joined hands with Gina. They strolled down the aisle hand in hand and were still clinging to each other when everyone reassembled thirty minutes later for the photos.

The photographer personally selected by Jennie clapped his hands to get everyone's attention. "Since the kids are getting antsy, we'll start with photos of the whole clan first."

He arranged the entire family, including spouses and children, and even Mitch's sister, Angie, and Luke's sister, Natalie. Next, he added Gina's parents, who took Sophia. Tears Gina had kept at bay started flowing.

"Hey," Derrick said. "What's wrong?"

"Nothing."

"Then why the tears?"

"Look at all of them." She shook her head as she counted everyone. "What have I done to deserve such a big, wonderful family?"

"We're the ones who have to work to deserve you, Mrs. Justice." Derrick thumbed her tears away and kissed her soundly amidst the hoots and whistles of his—*their*—family.

Breathless, Gina pulled back and peered into her husband's eyes.

"Are you still sure you want to be part of this family of hooligans?" he asked with that lopsided grin that sent her heart beating faster.

"Absolutely." She twined her arms around his neck. "As long as they don't come along on the honeymoon."

Derrick roared with laughter then lifted Gina,

slowly spinning her until her train twined around their legs. She laid her head on his shoulder and knew without any doubt that their life as a family would be as blessed as this moment.

* * * * *

Dear Reader,

Wow! I can't believe the Justice Agency series has come to an end. When I started the series five books ago, I didn't imagine the day that I'd have to say goodbye to this family that has touched my heart. And I have to admit, I'm feeling very sad at the farewell and yet honored to have been able to share their stories with you.

I hope you've enjoyed seeing these five brave family members work through issues in their lives to find their happily ever after with equally strong spouses. I've enjoyed every minute of writing about them and hope their faith struggles have lifted you up and encouraged you in your walk with God.

I love to hear from readers, and you can reach me through my website, www.susansleeman.com, or in care of Love Inspired Books at 233 Broadway, Suite 1001, New York, NY 10279.

## Questions for Discussion

1. Gina lived most of her life through the lens of her father's rejection. Is there something in your life that colors how you look at things?

2. Gina was able to let go of the hurt and pain her father brought to her life. Do you think she should've reconciled with him and given him another chance? If not, how would you have handled it?

3. Gina suffered so many losses in a short time and came out the other side strong and whole. Have you ever suffered tremendous loss, and how did you cope?

4. Gina's past experiences have led her to believe she can't trust men. Has anything in your life made you less trustful of others? If so, how has it changed your life?

5. When Gina's father continually rejected her, she blamed God and walked away from Him. Have you let anything come between you and God, and if so what did you do about it?

6. Derrick makes sure he keeps a tight schedule to prevent bad things from happening in his life.

Though time management is a positive trait, he's taken it to the extreme. Is there something you're doing to prevent a reoccurrence of a bad situation, and should you be letting it control your life?

7. Derrick blames himself for the loss of his parents. Is there anything in your life that you're taking blame for that you should let go?

8. Gina and Derrick decide to raise Sophia as their own child, waiting to tell her about her birth parents when she's old enough to understand. Do you think they made the right decision? Why or why not?

9. Which character in the story do you relate most to and why?

10. What about the whole Justice Agency series? Is there a particular character you really connected with and why?

11. Which book in the Justice Agency series did you like the most and why?

12. Through the Justice Agency series, Kat has been a defender of her siblings, watching to make sure they don't get hurt. Dani is the cheerleader, pointing out the positive. Cole gives wise advice. Ethan

leads the group and keeps them focused. Derrick keeps them on schedule. Do you see the people in your family playing similar roles? How does this dynamic make your family a cohesive group?

# LARGER-PRINT BOOKS!

## GET 2 FREE
## LARGER-PRINT NOVELS
## PLUS 2 FREE
## MYSTERY GIFTS

*Love Inspired*
# SUSPENSE
RIVETING INSPIRATIONAL ROMANCE

## Larger-print novels are now available...

LISLPDIR13R

# LARGER-PRINT BOOKS!

## GET 2 FREE LARGER-PRINT NOVELS PLUS 2 FREE MYSTERY GIFTS

*Love Inspired*®

### Larger-print novels are now available...

**YES!** Please send me 2 FREE LARGER-PRINT Love Inspired® novels and my 2 FREE mystery gifts (gifts are worth about $10). After receiving them, if I don't wish to receive any more books, I can return the shipping statement marked "cancel." If I don't cancel, I will receive 6 brand-new novels every month and be billed just $5.24 per book in the U.S. or $5.74 per book in Canada. That's a savings of at least 23% off the cover price. It's quite a bargain! Shipping and handling is just 50¢ per book in the U.S. and 75¢ per book in Canada.* I understand that accepting the 2 free books and gifts places me under no obligation to buy anything. I can always return a shipment and cancel at any time. Even if I never buy another book, the two free books and gifts are mine to keep forever.

122/322 IDN F49Y

| Name | | |
|------|--|--|
| | (PLEASE PRINT) | |

| Address | | Apt. # |
|---------|--|--------|

| City | State/Prov. | Zip/Postal Code |
|------|-------------|-----------------|

Signature (if under 18, a parent or guardian must sign)

### Mail to the Harlequin® Reader Service:
**IN U.S.A.:** P.O. Box 1867, Buffalo, NY 14240-1867
**IN CANADA:** P.O. Box 609, Fort Erie, Ontario L2A 5X3

**Are you a current subscriber to Love Inspired books
and want to receive the larger-print edition?
Call 1-800-873-8635 or visit www.ReaderService.com.**

\* Terms and prices subject to change without notice. Prices do not include applicable taxes. Sales tax applicable in N.Y. Canadian residents will be charged applicable taxes. Offer not valid in Quebec. This offer is limited to one order per household. Not valid for current subscribers to Love Inspired Larger-Print books. All orders subject to credit approval. Credit or debit balances in a customer's account(s) may be offset by any other outstanding balance owed by or to the customer. Please allow 4 to 6 weeks for delivery. Offer available while quantities last.

**Your Privacy**—The Harlequin® Reader Service is committed to protecting your privacy. Our Privacy Policy is available online at www.ReaderService.com or upon request from the Harlequin Reader Service.

We make a portion of our mailing list available to reputable third parties that offer products we believe may interest you. If you prefer that we not exchange your name with third parties, or if you wish to clarify or modify your communication preferences, please visit us at www.ReaderService.com/consumerchoice or write to us at Harlequin Reader Service Preference Service, P.O. Box 9062, Buffalo, NY 14269. Include your complete name and address.

LILPDIR13R

# *Reader Service*.com

## Manage your account online!

- Review your order history
- Manage your payments
- Update your address

> *We've designed
> the Harlequin® Reader Service
> website just for you.*

## Enjoy all the features!

- Reader excerpts from any series
- Respond to mailings and
  special monthly offers
- Discover new series available to you
- Browse the Bonus Bucks catalog
- Share your feedback

*Visit us at:*
**ReaderService.com**